SCORPIO

EDITED BY AUSTIN P. SHEEHAN,
NEEN COHEN & ALANNAH K. PEARSON

THE ZODIAC SERIES

The Zodiac Series is a collection of twelve speculative fiction anthologies, each focusing on one of the Zodiac signs. The anthologies feature short stories and poems inspired by each sign, and retellings of the various myths behind those signs.

#

Capricorn Aquarius Pisces

Aries Taurus Gemini

Cancer Leo Virgo

Libra Scorpio Sagittarius

#

The Zodiac Series has been produced by Aussie Speculative Fiction, and each anthology contains a diverse selection of tales by talented writers from Australia and New Zealand.

ISBN: 978-0-6450228-1-0

I AM SCORPIO

Zoey Xolton

\#

I am the Scorpion and my constellation is Scorpio.

My tarot card is Death; I am an insightful soul and loyal companion.

At my best I am brave, resourceful and passionate.

At my worst I am secretive, distrustful and jealous.

Fluid and balanced, like my element: Water, mine is a Fixed sign.

I appreciate truth, facts, deep friendship and grand ideas.

However, I dislike lies, passive individuals and ignorance.

I am ruled by Pluto, and am guardian to the second day of the week.

My colours are scarlet and black.

ZOEY XOLTON

About the Author:

Zoey Xolton is an Australian Speculative Fiction writer, primarily of Dark Fantasy, Paranormal Romance, and Horror. Her works have appeared in over one-hundred themed anthologies, with more due for publication!

She has recently celebrated the release of her debut short story collection Darkly Ever After. *You can find further details regarding her many publications on her website: www.zoeyxolton.com!*

CONTENTS:

FOREWORD

Sasha Hanton

Eighth sign of the zodiac, Scorpio represents the fixed water sign. Known for being one of the fiercest signs, Scorpio natives are ruled over by the dwarf planet Pluto.

The constellation of Scorpio has one primary myth that has a vast number of variations. As with all constellations of the zodiac, Scorpio has a Greek myth relating to its origin. Each telling of Scorpio's rise to the stars revolves around another constellation, Orion the hunter—the constellation which Scorpio is said to chase across the night sky. The story always involves a giant scorpion pursuing Orion, though depending on the retelling, the god or goddess that sends the giant scorpion after Orion, the reason for Orion's punishment, and the way in which Orion dies changes.

In one variation, Orion brags about being the best hunter there is and how he will kill every animal (which is a common theme in several versions) and when his boast reaches the Goddess of the Earth, Gaia, she is understandably upset. Gaia then creates the giant scorpion and sends him to kill Orion.

When the giant scorpion succeeds, as a reward for saving all animal life, Gaia makes him into a constellation. Orion is then placed into the sky as a constellation by either Zeus or Artemis.

Another common retelling of the myth involves the Goddess Artemis. It is suggested that Artemis was enamoured by Orion, causing her brother Apollo to become jealous and protective. Apollo then called upon the giant scorpion to chase Orion, and the great hunter flees into the sea. Attempting to save Orion's life, Artemis shoots an arrow at what she thinks is the giant scorpion, but it turns out to be Orion's head. Overseeing the whole thing Zeus comes in and places both Orion and the giant scorpion into the sky as constellations. There are many other alternative retellings to the myth, some involving the Pleiades or Eos (Goddess of Dawn), but in each variation, the giant scorpion either chases or kills Orion and both are placed into the sky.

Just as all signs of the zodiac bear a connection to Greek mythos, they all also share ties to cards in the Major Arcana of the Tarot. Scorpio is associated with the thirteenth card, Death. Whilst there is no imagery of a scorpion on the Death card this card does relate to Scorpio, through its connection to Planet Pluto which is named for the Roman God of the Underworld and Wealth—whose Greek counterpart is Hades. Just as Pluto's domain is recognised for not being solely a bad place as that's where wealth comes from, the Death card of the tarot has more dimensions than simply death.

FOREWORD

Represented by a skeleton knight holding a black banner adorned with the mystic rose—a symbol of life—riding upon a white horse across a field, in the distance there are two towers between which the sun shines and before him a king, child and girl kneel while a priest stands waiting with his hands clasped. The divinatory meanings for Death in the upright position are about transformation, birth and rebirth, whilst in the reversed it hails stagnation and inertia. Linking with the Death card symbolises the power of Scorpio natives to overcome and transform, capable of looking past the surface to find the truths beneath. Scorpios have the ability to change their pain into love.

Pluto is known as "The Great Renewer" in astrology for its association to the part of a person that demolishes for the sake of rebuilding and its power to bring forth hidden desires. For those born under its rule between October 23rd and November 21st it bestows authority, the ability to succeed on their own but to be capable of collaborating with others, an inquisitive (or suspicious) nature, patience, and great charm. However it may also drive those under its rule to be self-destructive.

Scorpios tend to be the sign most people are wary of. Like the scorpion that represents them, they have their own metaphorical poison stinger, and they don't forget any slights. Let the charms of this anthology enchant you but be cautious, you never know when they might strike you with the unexpected.

About the Author:

Sasha Hanton grew up in the tropics of Darwin, Northern Territory. From a young age, she devoured books and iced coffee, both of which she continues to intake on an almost daily basis. Now living on beautiful Bribie Island in Queensland, her time is split between writing and spoiling her puppy Miley.

Sasha, who has a Bachelor of Journalism from Bond University, has dabbled in the journalistic profession but finds fiction far more fascinating. Her first published work The Short Story Press Collection *draws on her love for a diverse range of genres and passion for short stories. Coming from a multicultural background (Eurasian) she aspires to make her writing inclusive for people from all walks of life and to bring a unique blend of eastern and western culture to her writing.*

Throughout her life, she has been a lover of history and mythology, and at any time will find some way to worm one or the other into her storytelling. When she's not writing or reading she can be found walking her dog and volunteering. You can keep up with her writing over on www.theshortstorypress.wordpress.com

SCORPION'S STING

Nikky Lee

The girl was dead. That much was clear as Scorpion scuttled across the hot sand. Face down, the girl's hair had spilt across the earth in dark, spider-web strands. Eagle, Ant and Coyote had already taken their fill; her eyes were hollow sockets, her rib cage cracked open to the sky.

"Died of thirst," Scorpion said, studying the body. Not a violent death as far as she could see. Her claws opened and closed on the air, tail poised high over her head. A breath of wind stirred the sand and the scorpion shifted, tilting her body into a question as she turned to the ghost huddled in the sand by the dead girl's feet.

"Why are you still here?" Scorpion asked.

The ghost girl raised her head, unwrapped her arms from her knees. Her skin was blotched and mottled in shades of blue, black and purple, just like Rattlesnake's. "You see me?" she whispered.

"I see you," Scorpion replied. "Though I should not. Why are you still here?" To Scorpion's mind, it was a pertinent question. The dead didn't stay without reason. She crawled towards the body, her eight legs picking across the sand to find cracked lips around a tongueless mouth. *Damned Coyote, taking all the best bits for himself.*

The ghost drew circles in the earth. Or tried to. Her fingers slipped through the grains as if they were made from cloud. "I died here," she said, sullenly.

"I can see that," Scorpion replied, picking her way through the dead girl's hair and up onto the head. She moved down the body, heading for the open rib cage. Perhaps there she'd be able to twist off some meat that hadn't hardened dry under the desert sun. "Most don't like to stick around to watch this."

The ghost's eyes, dark and ringed in shadow, followed Scorpion's progress, unflinching. "Where else can I go?"

Scorpion tilted her body again, tail twitching in surprise. "You don't feel it?"

"Feel what?"

"A pull . . ." Scorpion searched for the right words. "Onward. Away from here."

The ghost cocked her head, a faint furrow on her brow. There was a scar there too, a white ridge that cleaved one eyebrow in half. "Away to where?"

Scorpion threw her claws skyward, exasperated. "Somewhere not here." Truth be told, she didn't know. The Pull didn't apply to creatures of the Between. When their time came, they simply faded away. Scorpion had seen many fadings, thousands, perhaps millions, over the years. Saber-tooth, Auroch, and Dodo, among others. Their bodies had turned faint enough to see the desert and grasses through them. But Scorpion had not faded yet; her children were many and strong.

The ghost, for her part, had fallen quiet, her eyes glazed as she searched inward. "I don't feel anything," she said after a long pause.

Scorpion eyed her over a splayed rib as her claws worked a chunk of exposed flesh free. "Nothing?"

The girl shook her head, hugging her knees.

Intriguing. Scorpion abandoned her meal and approached the ghost. The girl's feet were bare and transparent, but when Scorpion poked one foot, the flesh was still solid. *Curious.* She scuttled up the girl's shin. The ghost's muscles tensed under her eight legs. At the girl's knees, where skin gave way to a sweat-yellowed dress, Scorpion paused to look into the girl's face. "What's your name, ghost?"

A pause. The wrinkle next to her scar deepened as the silence grew. "I don't know," the ghost said at last.

This was not so surprising. Their names were often the first thing the dead forgot. Scorpion considered calling for Human and letting him deal with this, but Human was even worse than Coyote. And he stomped about something chronic, which always made Scorpion's amour ache. No, she'd manage this incursion like she'd managed the others.

"What happened to you then?" she asked, gesturing a claw at the bruises on the girl's arms.

"I was . . ." The ghost closed her eyes, brow furrowing as she tried to remember. "Hurting. They hurt me. A lot." Her voice grew stronger and her eyes roved beneath her eyelids. "They said I should be thankful they took me in after Ma died. But they made me work. All day. With no water. Then she'd hit me and he'd watch." Her ghostly body quivered. "I ran away."

"I can see you did," Scorpion said. "Or that you tried to."

The girl looked to her corpse and she grew still, then dragged in a ghostly breath. "I didn't mean to die." The last word came out as a sob and she buried her face in her arms.

Scorpion rested her claws on the girl's arms. "And yet here you are." If she could've sighed, she would have. But her accordion lungs weren't made for that. Instead, Scorpion tapped first one leg, then another in a melancholy rhythm on the girl's skin. *A ghost with no pull. What to do, what to do.* "I could take you back. Not permanently," she added. "A brief visit."

The ghost's eyes met Scorpion's glittering black ones. "Why?"

Scorpion shrugged her claws—a move learned from Human at some point over the years. "To find your pull." She had thought the answer obvious, but the girl wasn't of the Between. She wouldn't—couldn't—know these things. "You can't stay here," Scorpion said. "It's not good. For you or the Between." Her back arched at a memory of a dog who'd stayed trapped in the Between too long. At the end, it hadn't been a dog anymore. Just hunger, eating everything that moved. It devoured Coyote three times before he learned not to stick his nose there. Once was enough for Scorpion. She shuddered, recalling those monstrous teeth crunching through her carapace. She might be immortal, but she still felt pain. Since then, she'd made a point not to let any ghost stay too long. "Well?" She prompted, sting quivering. The girl didn't have a choice—not if Scorpion had any say in it. But it would be easier if the girl agreed.

The girl's tear-streaked face took in the desert sands; the scrawny grasses dotted here and there. She wiped her eyes, squared her jaw, and gave a short nod. "Yes. I'll do it."

Thank the Between. "Good," Scorpion replied. If she could have smiled, she would have. Her tail arched, venom bulb tipped and ready. "This is going to sting."

She plunged her tail into the girl's arm.

The girl blinked open her corpse's dead eyes. "What is this?"

"A second chance," Scorpion said, clawing her way up the corpse's dress and onto her head. "Don't waste it."

"And this?" the girl asked, pinching a lock of hair before her face. It twisted and coiled in her fingers like a worm on a hook, its end arching into a pointed sting.

"Protection," Scorpion said and left it at that.

The girl nodded, writhing locks settling on her back.

She followed her own tracks, gait measured and unhurried as she picked her way back through the desert. Her shoes were worn through and filled with the desert sand. In the glaring midday sun, her skin cracked and her bruises took on a yellow hue. The smell of sour meat grew stronger, wafting up from her open ribs. Atop the girl's head, Scorpion surveyed the way before them. The passage the girl had taken before in her final hours stood out like stars in a night sky—a blaze of footprints to her Between eyes. With Scorpion's venom gluing the girl back into her shell, the ghost inside saw the way too. So Scorpion remained silent, leaving the ghost the task of plucking and pulling her skin and bones across the desert.

The tracks stretched on. And so they followed.

This world was similar to the Between. Same terrain, same clear blue sky, withered grasses and scraggily shrubs twisting out of the earth. But here, everything *moved*. Instead of still, belly-up bodies, ant trains crawled the ground and flies circled in their dozens. A pair of hawks glided overhead. There, a

10

scrawny rabbit darted back into its burrow. The world spun with life. Dizziness swirled through Scorpion's cephalothorax and she drew her senses away, turning her sight back to the Between. Her home hung there, perfectly overlaid on this world, a still and silent haze on the horizon.

Night had fallen by the time they reached the homestead. It was a tumbledown thing with one end of the porch caved in. Sand had scored the paint away years ago, except for the faintest flecks of white still remaining on the gate. The girl paused, hand on the threshold. Moonlight was kinder to her features than the harsh sun. Her bruises vanished into the shadows, as did the exposed cavity of her chest.

In the distance, Coyote's brethren yipped and howled.

"Go on," Scorpion urged, tapping a claw to the corpse's head.

The girl's hair twitched, the ends rising off her back, each lock turning stinger sharp.

With one hand on the gate, the girl hesitated. "I'm scared," she whispered.

"We're always scared," Scorpion replied. Something she had learned from her ages in the Between.

"Who?"

"Everyone."

The girl's hand tightened on the latch, steadying the shake in her fingers. She pushed open the gate and shuffled down the

11

overgrown path, then up onto the porch, scuffing her heels on the rough boards. She paused at the door and—just when Scorpion was about to remind her that her time in this world was only temporary—lifted a hand as if to knock, then curled her fingers around the doorknob.

The door popped opened. Unlocked.

"She always forgot to lock it," the corpse murmured, and Scorpion sensed the memory dart out of death's darkness like a flash of fish scales in a murky stream. With a long, low creak, the girl pushed the door wide. She listened, and Scorpion listened too. The house was still, but for a faint snore in its depths.

A boiler stove loomed in the kitchen, though the fire was out. The girl shuffled past a sitting room, worn rugs on the floor, a rocking chair in one corner, brown curtains blocking the windows. They turned into a hallway and the girl's eyes landed on the broken shards of a whiskey glass swept to one side of the passage.

Atop her head, Scorpion felt a tremor run up the girl's spine. Her broken body stiffened; hair curling into razors.

"You." The word hissed from the darkness of a doorway. "Come crawling back, eh?" A shadow shifted, lumbered onto its feet. A hand, viper quick, lashed out and snatched the girl's arm. A woman's face loomed out of the shadows, pale and with high cheekbones, bloodshot eyes, and lines around a

mouth set in a scowl. She might have been pretty, but her expression was enough to curdle milk.

The girl flinched, shrinking into herself—submission ingrained even in death.

"Little wench." The scent of whiskey rolled off the woman's breath. A finger stabbed into the girl's collar—any lower and it would have found open flesh. "A fox got into the coop because of you! Ronk has an udder infection because you didn't milk her—" She raised an empty whiskey bottle, threatening to bring it down on the girl's head.

Scorpion shifted, her tail arching.

The girl remained motionless but for her writhing hair.

"—my floors need sweeping. Get outside and—" The woman sniffed, her face distorting into a new, twisted variant of disgust. She covered her nose. "Ugh! You reek."

She stepped back, taking in the girl properly for the first time. Her gaze travelled down the torn flesh and broken ribs to the open abdominal cavity missing all those important organs necessary for life. The woman's face turned pale, the pinkness in her cheeks washing away. A half-gurgle rose from her throat. She staggered backwards, the whiskey bottle falling to the floor with a 'thunk'.

"God's mercy," she whispered.

"Pounce, girl!" Scorpion urged. This was prey ready for the taking. But the girl didn't pounce, though the ends of her hair

13

curled and quivered with the want. Instead, she kept her eyes focused on a second door down the hall. One step, then another, and the woman shrank through her bedroom doorway like a spider retreating down its burrow.

"Roland!"

The snore cut off mid-draw. "Huh?"

"Your gun, Roland! Get your gun. *Now.*"

Scorpion imagined the woman rousing her mate, pulling at his nightshirt, shoving the weapon into his hands and pushing him to the doorway.

"Be careful," Scorpion warned the girl. "They can't kill you, but they can break the bond holding you here. And I can't bring you back again." And if that happened, she'd become a problem for all of the Between.

The girl's hair twitched. Her gait jerked and jolted as she forced her stiff limbs to move faster. "I won't leave him." It came out nearly a growl as she pushed deeper into the hallway, past the woman's bedroom, aiming for the door beyond.

Curious. Scorpion dug her claws into the girl's hair. She was remembering more and more. A good sign. *Although . . .*

Footsteps thumped behind them: the woman and her mate, sounding for all the world like a pair of buffalos barrelling down the hall. Their vibrations shivered up the girl's body and into Scorpion's legs. A millennia of her children's memories filled her; thousands of feet tramping outside dens, collapsing

14

tunnels, crushing her children alive. *Humans. Always so oblivious.* Her claws opened and shut with a snap.

"Shoot her!" the woman shrieked. "The Devil's in her I tell you."

The man grappled with his shotgun, shoving rounds into it with shaky fingers. His red hair was tousled, sticking up on one side. He lifted the gun and squinted down the barrel. His face slackened, eyes drawn to the girl's exposed chest cavity. He sucked in a breath. "By God, it's—"

"I know. She's desert dead. Put a bullet in her head and be done with it."

"But, Mary—" the weapon lowered "—it's . . ."

"God damn it, Roland. I'll do it myself." She yanked the gun from him, swung it up, and fired.

The girl didn't evade. *Couldn't,* Scorpion guessed. *Her time is almost up.*

The bullet tore a hole through the girl's abdominal cavity.

The girl cocked her head, a little gasp of surprise echoing from her spirit. "I don't feel it," she said to Scorpion.

"Of course not. The dead don't feel pain." Scorpion tapped a leg on the girl's head. "You're wasting time. Best not dally."

The girl nodded, a movement that almost threw Scorpion from her hair, and turned for the second door.

15

Another bang. Another bullet tore into the wall, splintering wood.

"Just die!" Mary screamed, and levelled the gun again. She stopped as a keening, then a burbling, howling wail rose from the second room.

Ah, so that's it.

"Shit," Mary huffed.

"If she wants him, let her take him," Roland said, groping for Mary's arm and trying to pull her back.

Mary shoved him away. "He's *my* child."

"But," he floundered, "you don't even *want* him."

Mary spat at her feet. "I don't give two fucks if he dies tomorrow, but I'm sure as hell not giving *her* anything."

The girl's corpse shuddered, arms twitching as she strode for the couple. They cowered away, tripping over each other and falling to the ground.

Sprawled on the floor, the woman snatched the gun up again, ready to shoot. It emptied with a hollow click—nothing in the chamber.

The girl advanced on the couple, her hair snapping out, dark and deadly. She knocked the gun asunder from the woman's trembling arms and it clattered to the floor. The pair scrambled away.

"Have him then!" Mary cried. "Take him and get out!" She tripped over her cowering husband and they went down in a tangle of limbs. "Roland, you oaf! Get off."

Scorpion dropped to the girl's shoulder, scuttled down the blood-soaked dress and onto the floor. "Go," she said. "Find the child. Time is closing."

The girl managed a stiff nod and entered the second bedroom.

Scorpion closed in on the writhing couple. Perhaps she should have let Human deal with them, but their bickering had ground her temper raw, every oafish *thud-thudding* jarred through her body. She rubbed her jaws together, issuing a soft hiss. This had gone far enough.

She struck.

Mary jerked upright, howling and clutching at her ankle. Her mate furrowed his brow then he too yelped as Scorpion's sting found home in his thigh. Spitting curses, they rounded on Scorpion crouched in the shadows.

"Damn insect, I'll squash you flat," Mary snarled.

Scorpion twitched her arachnid laugh. "I think not."

Curled on the floor, the pair gawked. They'd heard her. Of course they had.

If Scorpion could have grinned, she would have. Instead, she snapped her claws and drummed a leg on the floor like a spider testing its web. The magic in their veins responded.

17

Twitching, twisting and roaring to life. *Good, good.* Scorpion let the thrill ride through her. Small she might be, and old beyond belief, but even Human feared her sting—as right he should. Now it was his children's turn.

Mary gasped, then folded into herself, clothes going limp.

Roland screamed, eyes bulging as Scorpion's beady eyes swung to him.

"Oh yes, you too," she said.

Roland gasped as he shrank into his bedclothes, becoming smaller, then smaller again—his bones cracking, breaking and remaking.

A moment later, two young scorpions—small and soft shelled—scuttled out of the folds of clothing. They hissed at Scorpion, arched their tails, voices chittering in her head.

"What did you do to us? Turn us back!"

Scorpion rounded on them, her claws snapping shut just short of Mary's newly-armoured head. "Don't test me," Scorpion said, opening her claws again. Next time, she wouldn't miss.

"You can't do this." Roland stomped his legs unevenly. It would take him a while to learn to use them properly, but he would learn. Or he would die. Scorpion wasn't too concerned which.

"You are my children now, I can do what I like." Scorpion clicked her jaws. "Cruelty is not befitting in my children. A life as my kindred will teach you better. Now go, before I change my mind."

Mary's tail thrashed, fisting at the air. *"We won't forget this. I'll—"*

Scorpion's claws lashed, viper quick, snagging one of Mary's forelegs and dragging the youngster close. *"Enough,"* she hissed. And with a crunch, she ripped Mary's leg clean off.

Mary screamed, her jaws clacking together. *"My leg! My leg! She fucking took my leg Roland!"*

"Mary! Oh God!" Roland scuttled about, tripping over his own feet, panic shivering up and down his one-inch stature. *"Oh God, oh God."*

"Quiet!" Scorpion silenced them both as only a mother could. Reaching out, she seized the magic in their bodies and froze them in place. *"I* am your mother now." She arched her tail. "And I've grown weary of the sight of you. Get out, before I give you a real sting to complain about."

The two youngsters retreated to the shadows, scuttling along the skirting boards, grumbling as they went. A footstep rattled the floorboards at Scorpion's back. The girl. She carried a bundle in her arms. A babe peeked out, bright eyes and a fluff of brown hair.

With a shrug of her claws—Scorpion's version of a sigh—she clambered back up the corpse's tattered dress and onto her shoulder. "You can't take him with you."

"I know," the girl replied.

"You got somewhere in mind then?"

There was a long moment before the girl forced a nod.

"Is it far?"

A stiff shake of her head.

"Good. You haven't long left."

They returned to the desert, this time forging a new path. The girl's pace had slowed, her feet dragged, and Scorpion felt her wrestling with the dwindling magic. On the horizon, a sliver of pink heralded the approaching dawn.

"Almost there," the girl whispered. "Almost there." She stumbled over a rise and there below, nestled beside on oak, lay a small cottage, a corral and barn to one side. The girl surged forward, clutching the babe to her rendered flesh. A shudder ran through her, and she stumbled and fell onto her knees.

Scorpion plopped to earth, sure this was the end. Instead, the girl crawled, dragging the bundle the final few feet and depositing it on the wooden porch as if the baby were made of glass.

"The Morrisons were always kind to me," the girl said, bowing to kiss the child's head. "He'll be safe here."

Scorpion quivered as the last traces of her magic dissolved. "Time's up," she said.

The girl sat back and looked up at the fading stars. "Anna."

"What?"

"My name." Her hollowed eyes turned on Scorpion. "I remembered. Thank you." Then her chin dropped to her chest and the corpse slumped. Empty.

As Scorpion crouched there in vigil, the girl's skin flaked away, bones shrivelling into dust until all that was left was a small mound of debris.

And then it was done.

On the porch, the babe began to cry.

With a flit through the Between, Scorpion re-emerged in the world atop the rise, just as candlelight flared behind the cottage window. A soft vibration on the sand made her turn. "Human," she acknowledged. The figure—long and lanky as ever—crouched down beside her. "Took your sweet time."

He winced. "Can't be everywhere, Scorpion." He sighed, long and heavy. "But you have my thanks."

Scorpion snapped a claw. "Do it yourself next time. I'm getting tired of cleaning up after everyone else's children."

Human scratched the bristles on his chin. "But you've got to admit, you are rather good at it."

"Prick."

"Grump."

Human grinned into the silence. "Come on." He offered his palm to Scorpion. "I hear Coyote's got himself into some trouble again."

Scorpion bristled. "Help him yourself, I've been up all night."

Human shrugged, gaze drifting down to the Morrisons, exclaiming over the baby below. "I guess you've earned it."

When no reply came, he turned. "Scorpion?" The space beside him was empty but for the faint imprint of her armour in the sand. Returned to the Between. He sighed again, sinking into himself.

"I owe you one," he whispered into the dawn.

About the Author:

Nikky grew up as a barefoot 90s child in Perth, Western Australia, before moving to New Zealand in 2016. By day she works as a professional content writer and by night authors speculative fiction, often burning the candle at both ends to explore fantastic worlds, mine asteroids and meet wizards. Her creative work has appeared in magazines, on radio and in anthologies around the world. Her debut novel, The Rarkyn's Familiar—*a dark tale of a girl bonded to a monster—will be published by Parliament House Press in 2022.*

You can find her online at:
W:nikkythewriter.com | T:@NikkyMLee | F:nikkythewriter

CRISIS OF FAITH

Jo Mularczyk

It really worked!

Julia looked around at the wooden pews and the distorted rainbows of afternoon light cast by the stained-glass windows. The familiarity was confronting. She was standing in her childhood church, stage of much guilt and teenage angst. Why had St Anne's been the first place to pop into her head? A therapist would probably have a field day with that one!

Clutched tight in her hand was the contraption that represented ten years of her life, thousands of dollars and countless lost relationships. It was the symbol of both her ostracism and her brilliance. Oh, how the scientific community had scoffed when she'd first presented her idea. They had labelled it an abomination, and worse, told her it would never work. She had been the subject of mocking and ridicule. They had called her Jules Verne.

And now here she was, vindicated creator of a displacement nodule that could transport a person to any location instantaneously. It had finally worked—after persistent testing and adjustment—which is how she now stood across the country in the pulpit of St Anne's staring at a multitude of candles laid by blindly faithful parishioners. Her derisive thoughts betrayed her allegiances. Julia had turned away from her childhood faith in her adult years, choosing instead to worship at the altar of science. She knew 'how' she came to be standing here, but not 'why'.

"Okay, this is no time to examine your crisis of faith," she muttered. "Let's see what this thing can really do."

Julia took a deep breath and tightened her grip on the nodule. "The Eiffel Tower," she announced imperiously.

Just like the last time, the nodule heated up in her hands and a tingling started in her palms. It radiated throughout her body like tiny jolts of electricity. Her breathing sped up and her heart raced. A tiny voice inside tried to question how many times her body could withstand these stresses, but she silenced it. Her surroundings gradually faded out of focus and, at the last moment, a priest appeared with his mouth agape. She stifled the urge to wave.

The next moment, light was piercing her eyelids. She opened them to a bright Parisian morning, the Eiffel Tower looming in front of her.

"Julia," she whispered to herself, "you bloody genius! Nobel Prize here I come. In fact . . ." She grinned mischievously as she thought about the physics convention happening today in London. A group of her peers were meeting to fawn over each other and present their latest theories and dissertations. She could imagine the looks on their smug faces when she materialised in the middle of the convention hall, displacement nodule in hand. Her mother had always said that she had a sting in her tail. Well, it was time to use it. She had been scorned after all, and there was no point leaving the idiom unfulfilled. She took an irrational pleasure in proving her mother right in this one observation about her.

But first, she had time to indulge in a little sightseeing.

"When in Paris," she said with a manic laugh.

Julia wandered towards the Eiffel Tower, but was so busy admiring the displacement nodule that she tripped on a stone. Stumbling forward, she tightened her grip on the nodule.

"Oh hell!" she cursed.

Her eyes widened in fear as a familiar tingling started in her palms . . .

About the Author:

Jo enjoys writing in different genres for a range of audiences. Her stories and poems appear in magazines and anthologies including: Fire Burn, Cauldron Bubble by Bloomsbury UK; US magazine Cricket; The School Magazine; One Surviving Story by ICOE Press; fourW thirty's New writing: Pearl; Wonderment by Poetica Christi; Zinewest publications; Short and Twisted by Celapene Press; anthologies by Black Hare Press; and Storm Cloud Publishing publications. An earlier version of this story was published in Daily Science Fiction as Mad Science.

In 2020 Jo won the Mayoral Creative Writing Prize and the December Press 53-word story competition.

Jo shares the joy of writing through creative writing workshops, student mentoring and co-authoring with the student literacy program Littlescribe, www.littlescribe.com.

Jo lives in Australia with her husband and three children. Follow @ www.facebook.com/jo.mularczyk.author www.instagram.com/jo_mularczyk_authorpage/

THE ENDLESS CHASE

Tee Linden

The doe watched me at my campfire. She slinked through the cypress trees, her perfect, pale hide near glowing in the firelight. I sat on a felled tree and watched her from the corner of my eye.

It was winter. The winds off my father's sea were harsh that year and when I warmed my hands on the radiant heat of the fire, I could see the age in them. Even in those early days. No longer the hands of a young man. My knuckles ached more often than not.

The doe neared the campfire, as though taunting. Challenging me to pick up the still-strung bow at my heel. To nock the arrow. To shoot. My hunter's hands twitched. I knew the arrow wouldn't fly true. It couldn't. It was useless to try. It was madness to try. Dangerous, even.

Sirius sat at my side. He wasn't much more than a puppy then. My favourite. The bravest and fastest of all my dogs. Even he whimpered at the eerie doe with the rest of the pack. He curled his tremoring body against my feet.

The doe stalked. As fast as I could, I snatched up my bow and nocked an arrow. By the time the arrow was loosed, the doe had disappeared into the trees, melting into the deep shadows cast by the firelight.

As expected.

I smiled to myself. "Missed you again," I called, setting my bow down and my hand on Sirius' head to calm him.

I did not hear the change. I never did.

Her voice unpeeled from the trees and slithered towards me, accompanied by the sound of cicadas buzzing at the edges of her words. "Do you expect your arrow will ever fly true, Orion?"

"No," I said to the fire.

I was still wary around her then, though it's strange to think now. I had heard the stories of her. The first time I'd ever seen her, a doe as pale as snow, I had hunted her for days. Until my feet were blistered and I had no arrows with which to shoot.

"You knew the shot would not land before you loosed," she said, bringing the scent of night flowers as she drew near.

"Yes."

"Then why shoot?"

"That's part of the chase, isn't it?"

Silver sandaled feet stood beside me. Her shins were bare, pale as the inside of a shell. She wore a silver linen chiton and her cloak was deerskin. I risked a glance up to find her watching me with eyes the colour of brushed silver coin. A faint glow ebbed from her skin, like the moon behind clouds, and her black hair was braided with delicate links of chain. Her face was both ancient and ageless in the way of all Olympians. Artemis. Goddess of hunting, wild nature and chastity. Perfect and inhuman. Pitiless and beautiful.

"And what will happen," she asked, "if there comes a day you catch me?"

"I expect you'll kill me," I said airily.

That pleased her, a smile cracking the moon of her face.

She held her white wood bow, and I nodded to it. "Is the hunting good tonight?"

"Good enough even your arrows may find target," she taunted.

I took her teasing with good nature. Truth was, Artemis knew my skill at the hunt. It was why she spared me that first night. My relentlessness impressed her. Though far from the perfection of a goddess, I was known for those skills. Hunting. Shooting. Tracking. They had served me well and ill, in equal measure.

The two of us moved into the trees, my hunting dogs following.

We hunted like that for years, a pack, sneaking through the shadowy oak and juniper that grew over the mountains. She would come every other night. Mostly as herself. Sometimes as the glowing doe, beautiful and impossible to catch. We challenged one another. Shooting games. This deer, that boar. The chase. We both loved the chase. I think that's why we got along so well.

She admired my sight. It was far superior even to hers. My sight was a gift from Eos, the dawn goddess. I could spot a flea jumping from a boar's back a hundred yards away. A good talent for a hunter. And I admired her. I still do.

She's graceful, Artemis. She flows like water. Watching her nock and shoot is always a great pleasure, the movement eased by thousands and thousands of repetitions. Like watching a skilled hand at a lyre or a master work flat marble into lip and cheek and hair.

Always, she flips back the deerskin cloak and raises her bow in one fluid motion, silver tipped arrow at the ready. Her pale muscled arms grow taut. Her grey eyes narrow but never blink. Her stern lips thin when she concentrates, and she becomes still.

Then her moonlight arrow flies true and straight. Always.

I was used to godhead, yes, I am the son of a god. But skill and prowess filled every line of her body. My godhead bestows certain gifts, speed and strength and an unsinkable body, but it was nothing compared to Artemis. Comparing our talent was like comparing a grain of sand to blown glass.

That night, I watched her take a great leap off a rock, her deerskin cloak flying, nocking mid-air and shooting at a swooping owl. Artemis landed on the grass with a roll, and a moment later, the owl fell from the sky and pattered to the clover, a silver arrow struck through its skull.

"I have never seen such a shot!" I blurted in the darkness.

Artemis turned to look at me. Her features were hard and beautiful with pride. "Do not be surprised at my skill, Orion. My arrows never miss."

And she was right.

Every morning on that island, Sirius and I rose and made our pilgrimage to either the shore or the high mountains so I could watch Eos, the dawn goddess, untangle the night from the sky with her rosy-tipped fingers. The birds would chirp to her, as I settled into a seat on the sand, or tree, or rock. I always awaited Eos. I always touched the shafts of burnt skin on either side of my eyes when I first felt the dawn slip over me; my own private ritual.

I'd once been blinded by a traitorous king, and Eos had taken pity on me at the watery edge of the world. She'd restored my sight, refined it to rival a hawk's, and every day I thanked her.

After Eos had settled back into slumber, I moved back into the forest. I fletched arrows. Fed my dogs. Prepared camp or packed it up.

I remember it was noon, my shadow was small, and I was skinning goat when the world suddenly froze around me. The songs of the birds were silenced and every leaf in every tree stilled all at once. I gave a deep, laboured sigh, and stood with bloodied hands to face my interloper. It was not the first time he'd visited me, and it wasn't the last. But it was the most important.

He stepped in from nowhere at all, splitting the air like a flash of light. The twin sun to his sister moon. Apollo.

He was brown-skinned and sculptured where she was pale and soft, and his hair was silky gold where hers was thick black. His eyes were wide, blue afternoon sky. Even the ebony bow on his back was a perfect reflection of her white wood.

A gilded wreath shimmered in the sunlight, crowning a beautiful face filled with barely covered malice. "Orion." He said my name in a way that would send other mortals running. "I told you to leave this island."

"My home, you mean," I said.

"I told you to leave," he repeated.

While I had no wish to anger the god of light and prophecy, he hadn't left me much choice. "And I told you it is my home."

He did not like that answer. The very air crushed me down, tasting of metal as it forced me to my knees. Sirius whimpered, pressed down into the nettled grass beside me.

Apollo approached me, moving like silk in the breeze. His face shined, placid as he watched me choke and writhe beneath a great boulder of nothing.

Apollo's sulky, spiteful wrath was legendary.

Once, when trying to seduce Cassandra of Troy, Apollo had offered her his gift of prophecy. But when she refused him her bed, he'd spat in her mouth, cursing her so no matter how many true prophecies she spoke, no one would ever believe her.

Upsetting Apollo was the last thing I had mind to do. But the island didn't belong to Apollo. In title, this was my island. Artemis was its patron. And I had her protection. So eventually he released me, and my dog, and I stood, resettling my chiton and trying to quell the rage that grew like wild weed within. It held no use. It never did. Apollo watched me, empty and beautiful. His presence always filled me with burrs. I couldn't wait for him to be gone once more.

"She will not petition for immortality for you," he announced. "Zeus would never approve it. You are nothing, Orion, and you have done nothing to deserve being remembered. Your own father does not remember you exist."

Looking back, I think the cruelty was unintended and conversational. Apollo had lived thousands of years with no understanding of pain, and so unleashed it without realising. But at the time, I felt it like a spear thrust deep into my belly.

Poseidon had hundreds of byblows. And I was born mortal; the immortality of gods made time difficult for them. In my life, I spoke with my father only three times. Each time I had to remind him who I was, and even then he only looked at me like a messenger of inconvenience.

"I have no wish to be immortal," I told Apollo.

"You are renown for your hunting skills. You are the son of a god, and a prince of Crete. She cannot improve your favour in what little life you have left."

I frowned. "I do not want anything from her."

He scoffed at that. Olympians are always jockeying for power and pride. Holding it, fighting for more, seeking retribution for any lost or injured. Especially Artemis and Apollo. I had heard a story that Niobe, a queen of Thebes, had boasted she was superior to the twin's mother, Leto, because Niobe bore fourteen children to Leto's two. For that insignificant injury, Apollo and Artemis had hunted each of Niobe's children and shot them, one by one.

I imagine Apollo couldn't understand that I wanted nothing from Artemis. Least of all power.

The god approached me, his gold-sandaled feet weightless on the grass. "Artemis will not lie with you," he told me.

I cleared my throat. "Perhaps we just enjoy each other's company, Apollo."

Apollo looked like I'd spat in his mouth. "My sister does not enjoy the company of men. She never has."

I looked to him, in his jealous, interminable rage, and decided not to point out that he might be the reason why. "Mere mortals like myself who look upon your sister are transformed into deer and ripped apart by dogs," I said instead.

He stepped closer to me, peering down at me with blue eyes flashing cold. The gilded wreath in his hair, laurel wood, caught the sun like a still lake, flashing sharp as a blade.

More stories.

Daphne, a river nymph Apollo had pursued so viciously, had turned herself into a laurel tree to escape his advances. He'd taken wood from her desperate escape to make the wreath that sat atop his perfect head, and though there was much about Apollo to find unsettling, it was that wreath that unsettled me the most. The sight of the wreath always twisted my gut.

"It is unseemly for the goddess of chastity to spend nights with a mortal."

I disliked this whole conversation, and my skin prickled from being in his presence. I do not know how Artemis had withstood this for so long. I still don't.

"Your sister is a goddess," I said. Warning slipped into my words, though I knew it shouldn't be there. "She can make her own choices."

"If you seduce her," Apollo persisted, "you risk her vow to Zeus. And so her."

"If you are so invested in chastity," I glanced at his wreath, petrified body of a desperate nymph, "you could always take the vow yourself. Save some would-be laurel trees."

He stared at me, hollowed of empathy. I wondered at the time if he would kill me, despite his sister's protection. I had overstepped the crawling space reserved at a god's feet and I regretted it immediately.

The fallen leaves raised from the ground, floating upwards. The ropes of my intestines pressed up against my stomach, and my stomach to my lungs. I could not breathe, his entire being crushing every inch of mine. I watched him bug-eyed and silent, suspended in airlessness, about to drown in my own sour bile.

When he spoke again his voice had changed, growing deep, every word shaking the foundations of the earth itself. "Orion. I have a prophecy for you. Your death will be delivered by the sea." His smile was empty and unendingly cruel. "I will be there when it happens. I will laugh as I watch you die."

He flashed away, a lightning strike of anger. The leaves settled. The sound of birds returned. And I could breathe again.

I fell to my hands and knees on the nettled grass and vomited.

"Your father rages," Artemis said, as we stood atop a mountain looking out over the roiling sea.

I continued building a fire. "Why does he rage?"

"Polyphemus was killed," Artemis said.

"Who is that?" I asked.

She blinked, expressionless. "Your brother. The cyclops."

"Oh," I said, scratching Sirius' broad head as my loyal boy sat by my feet. The dog was older by then, no longer a puppy, and he'd outlived many of my other dogs. "I never think about Poseidon's children as my siblings. It seems strange."

"You do not mourn?"

"How can I mourn someone I don't know?" Even as I said it, I realised I could. Since Artemis told me of Daphne, I had mourned for she of the laurel wood. Yet I felt nothing for Polyphemus. "How old was he?"

"Older than me."

"That's old," I said with a smile.

She smiled back, shining like the moon. My stomach flipped.

It wasn't the first time I had felt that familiar bite of ardour in her presence. Love came easy but fickle for me. It flowed and ebbed like the tide. Love was just another chase. Eos. Merope. The nereids that slipped from the sea, seeking me in my youth. All of them were easily loved and easily left. The feeling that filled me, looking at Artemis, was faded with age and use. I appreciated it for what it was, even if I could never act on it. I had no urge to be turned into a stag and gored by my own dogs.

She turned away, looking out over the sea again. I remembered Apollo's prophecy, turning it over in my mind. I couldn't imagine how the sea could deliver my death. Poseidon might not know me, but still; I was the son of the god who commanded the ocean. It gave me certain skills. I could swim from island to island without failure, without sinking; it's how I had swum to Eos at the edge of the watery world for her to restore my sight.

"Speaking of brothers," I cleared my throat. "Yours came to see me."

She sighed. "Apollo, I presume. He has been in my ear about you, like a giant, gold gnat. He is prone to jealousy."

"Jealousy," I repeated.

"Yes. Always. Since he was a baby. It was the nine days I had alone with our mother, when Hera banned Eileithyia from my mother's side." At the shake of my head, she clarified. "Eileithyia is the goddess of childbirth. Without her, Apollo was stuck inside. Eileithyia whispered to me on the winds, teaching me midwifery as to deliver him."

"As an infant. In nine days," I laughed.

"Yes," she said, fine chin raised. "There was no one else on Delos. Only me, and my mother. And then Apollo. The three of us against all the gods in Olympus and the Underworld. Against Hera herself, who wanted us dead. And still does. She always tries to find one way or another to remove our godhead."

When she talked of her mother or brother, she softened in a way that escaped the stories. When people spoke of Artemis, she was unbreakable as a shield, and as heartless as her silver-tipped arrows. The coldness makes a stronger goddess. A stronger story.

"Hera can remove your godhood?" I asked.

"Zeus can. Hera searches for a reason."

I thought on that, and on Apollo's words. *You risk her vow, and so her.*

Artemis looked to me. "What did he say?"

I didn't want to tell her about us arguing over her vow of chastity. Artemis was lenient with me, that wouldn't be denied, but the whole conversation seemed ripe for humiliation on her behalf. "A prophecy," I said instead.

A stillness hardened her, like freeze on a lake. "What kind of prophecy?"

"He said the sea will deliver my death," I said, saving her the rest of it.

She frowned. "You are a son of Poseidon. How could the sea kill you? You who can swim to the edge of the world? Who cannot drown or tire in the waves?"

"I don't know."

She continued frowning, watching me light the fire. "Well," she said stiffly. "You will just remain here. Never return to the sea and you will never die."

I laughed at that. She seemed so young at that moment. Endlessly young. Age brings wisdom, but Artemis was a goddess; she never aged. "I am mortal."

She blinked, expressionless and uncomprehending. The fire caught, scenting the air with burning oak.

"I will die," I said. "Of something. We all do."

I was at peace with that, in a way most mortals weren't. Looking back, I think it was because I loved the hunt. Death was a necessity.

But Artemis looked disconcerted, as though this has never crossed her mind. She was on her feet, grabbing her bow before I could stand. "I must go." She disappeared, lighting the night like starfall, disappearing from the world as easily as her brother.

The Goddess of the Hunt didn't return the next night, which wasn't rare. Then she didn't return for a few, which was rarer. Then a moon passed, waxing then waning. And still, she didn't return. Then another moon cycled. Then again. And a year passed. The baby kestrels lost their fluff, grew sleeker and flew. And then again, the next year. The olive trees bloomed and produced green, firm fruit, which ripened and dropped. And then again, the next year.

Eventually, heart-sore, I caught goats and brought them to her temple in the outskirt forests to sacrifice in her name. The gods can hear you at their temples, even on Olympus. Even Artemis, even during the day when she was deaf to me. The priestesses watched me from the temple, veiled and silent. They approached with garlands for the animals so I could dress them for her altar.

She never answered me. I stopped taking goats to her temple, and the wound of her abandonment slowly closed.

It was more than a few years later, when Artemis stepped out of nothing. Sirius and I were making our way up the White Mountains in the early morning, our daily pilgrimage to thank Eos. Much slower those days due to the stiffness that had gathered in my boy's aging joints. The flashing arrival of the goddess cracked the purpling sky. I flinched but didn't slow my journey, unable to think of anything to say, feeling my anger and hurt come to boil.

She strode along beside me for a moment, keeping pace, her face drawn tight as a bow. It was strange to see her under the chirping of dawn birds. I had never seen her so late.

41

"Apollo refuses to explain his prophecy," she said.

"Hello," I responded, the wound of her abandonment opening fresh and oozing.

She looked at me, confused, and I realised she didn't know how long she'd been gone. My father looked at me the same way when I'd told him who I was. She was a goddess, and not only did she not have to explain her sudden absence to me, she hadn't even noticed it. If I looked older to her, she didn't say anything.

I realised I was chasing a doe I could never catch and shook my head at myself, at my self-inflicted injury.

"He wants you dead." She told me this plainly, as if discussing the weather. "He has told me to kill you many times. He is in a fit."

I said nothing. What was there to say? The discussion had closed years ago. She had left, and I had grown older, and I no longer even thought about Apollo's prophecy. But here she was, picking up the thread of conversation as though we'd been discussing it only the day before.

"I am patron of this island," she said with anger lurking in her voice. "And of you. The only person who can kill you here is me. He is angry about that. But he can continue to rage. And you will continue to live."

I knew this was untrue even as she said it. At that time, my hair was already greying. My skin had thinned and sagged. "Mortal life is not endless," I reminded her.

"Apollo has prophesised your death," she said. Her words were short and sharp. "If the sea delivers your death, and you never again touch the sea, then you can never die."

Not dying seemed simple for a goddess, I suppose. Not so for a mortal. Death comes for us all even when the gods do not wish it.

We never spoke of Apollo again.

Artemis visited more often after that, and I never questioned her years of absence. It meant nothing to her, and I was glad to have her presence again. I had been across the world; I had swum its breadth, seen its many shores of sand and stone and hard-faced cliffs. I had met many people, but I had always felt an outcast. It's why I ended up on my island, alone, with a dog for a companion. An oddness about demigods was not uncommon, or so I came to know, much later in my years. We are not really anything, not gods but not normal humans either. We fit nowhere.

But Artemis soothed something fractious in me. There was a sameness about us. So, we hunted which always pleased us both. We challenged each other to shooting games. I showed her the baby kestrels, and she marvelled over the tiny fluffy bodies that would become such sleek, master-hunters.

Artemis and I argued only once in all the time we spent together on that island. It was years later, when she arrived while I was building a pyre on the shore for Sirius. His old, greyed body was wrapped in linen, laying on the sand, and my throat was thick with the pain of his loss.

Artemis appeared and, without a moment's pause for my grief, she howled with anger. The sound crackled like lightning, and the air rushed from me, emptying itself until I was on my knees on the shore, shells digging into my shins as I clutched at my throat. Sand stung at me like tiny wasps, slicing and burning my skin.

Anger made her fine features ragged and incandescent, and I could finally see in her the Artemis that felled gods on a boast, that turned men into stags for dogs to rip to shreds.

"What are you doing?" she shrieked, like knives in my ears.

"Artemis!" I choked. My face blistered in the heat of it. "Can't breathe!"

The air rushed back into my lungs and I gulped at it greedily, like a desert-traveller stumbling on an oasis. Sand fell like rain, pattering into my hair, against the raw skin of my shoulders.

She grabbed my arm and pulled me up, dragged me into the forest, where she glowed in rage.

My anger mirrored hers. I jerked my arm away. "Never do that again!" I cried, at the goddess who had never taken a direction in her life.

"I never took you for a fool," she hissed, her face twisted. "Do you wish to die? The sea delivers your death."

"I didn't go in the sea," I snapped.

"You were mere steps from it!"

She was furious, but the fury was mixed with shock and fear too. Emotions I'd never seen on her stern face before. She was scared. For me.

"I was dry," I said. "On the sand. I haven't been in the sea in years."

"Apollo's prophecies are riddles. He may not mean drowning and you told me yourself; nereids slip from the sea to find you."

I laughed at that absurdity, even in my sorrow over Sirius, even with blood drying in tracks from my ears. "You believe some soft nereid is going to slip from their feasts in the golden palace just to murder me?"

She blinked. Then, she laughed as well, jittery with relief. "No," she admitted after a moment. "They would not dare." A begrudging smile slipped across her lips, stealing her weakened expression. The tension between us settled to the forest floor.

She refused me the beach, as well the sea. The goddess herself collected Sirius' wrapped body and convinced me to build my pyre at the top of the mountain instead of the shore. She carried him and I rebuilt the pyre. It took all night, and as the flames gathered, Artemis asked me if I wanted him laid to rest in the night sky.

"You can put Sirius in the sky?"

The flames that burnt my boy to ash lit Artemis and I both.

"I can," she said. "He will always be there, then. Chasing game through the stars."

My throat tightened and my face felt sodden with unshed tears. I remember that moment. Her pity and her kindness. "I would like that."

She just nodded, silver eyed and silent. We waited until the flames dwindled and then stood to watch Eos' pink hands of dawn unravel the night. Artemis observed me greet Eos, my daily ritual, with a nod and a touch to my scars.

"Why did the king blind you?" she asked.

"I wanted an impossible prize, so he set me an impossible challenge."

"The prize was his daughter," Artemis said. She knew the story. Of course, she knew. But she had never asked about Merope before.

My lips pressed together. "Yes. He tasked me with clearing his island of all beasts. He thought I would never complete it. And, if I am honest, neither did I. But I did."

"If you thought the task beyond you, why did you try?"

46

"Why do I hunt the goddess doe when I know I cannot catch her?" I said with a soft smile. "Because it is in me; that need to hunt. It is part of who I am. And when he challenged me, I couldn't refuse. What I should have seen was that he *thought* it was impossible. He didn't want me to marry his daughter. I should have recognised that, and realised every beast I killed was a step closer to my own destruction. I didn't. I was young. I killed each beast I laid eyes on."

"Did his daughter wish to marry you?" Artemis asked, watching the sky blush.

"She said she did. But a hunter is not a good match for the daughter of a king, and I am not a good match for anybody." I shrugged. "So when I completed his impossible task, he blinded me and told the people of Chios that I tried to flee with Merope."

"Why not kill him?"

"I thought about it. For years. It burned in me, that rage. Especially when I was young. That anger consumed my sightless days. I wasted years on that anger, dreaming of his death."

"What changed?"

I sighed. "I returned. After Eos restored my sight, I saw how the king had greyed. Merope had married. And all the animals were gone. Not the farm animals of men, but every other beast was gone from that island. I walked the hills. They were silent, and dead."

She watched me. "I do not understand."

I scratched my fingers through my hair, unsure how to explain. "I love the hunt, Artemis. The chase. They are as much me as my fingers and toes. But the hunt must end in death and so I must be careful where I direct my skills. He was an old man. Merope was a mother and a wife. When I saw what my hunting left, nothing but silence, I realised I must not hunt that which I don't want dead."

The sun rose but Artemis didn't leave. I was aware of it, because when the sun was high, Apollo could listen with all the sky.

"You were worried the hunt would consume you," Artemis said. "And her."

I nodded slowly. We always had so much common ground, she and I. We stepped in each other's footprints. "I could hunt everything." Those words echo even now. "I could hunt the entire world. I could kill every beast on this Earth. I think I realised that, when I returned to Chios with murder on my mind and saw the nothing I'd left behind. That endless, creature-less silence has stayed with me. It could so easily spread. And I didn't want to be the man who kills all he sees."

Daylight settled strangely on her. She lost her iridescence. She became flat. Like a stone carving erected at her temple. "You decided not to be the man who kills all he sees," she reflected. "Can one truly give that power up?"

"I did."

She looked out across the lightening sky, expressionless. "The other gods, they are always looking for a reason to knock me from Olympus. To make me mortal. So I can live and, therefore, die. They are jealous and cruel. They force me to guard my godhood endlessly, lest they take it from me."

Her gaze fell on our feet. "I must rise to every challenge, every slight, in case they find weakness. I must show them none. And so I am welcome nowhere, just as my mother was when she bore us."

The three of us against all the gods in Olympus and the Underworld.

I felt an echo of that in myself, though I would never dare to presume I knew what an ancient god could feel. So I said nothing.

She looked at me, weariness weighing heavy in all the features of her face. Tired, in a way no goddess should be. Her silver eyes were on me, unblinking and waiting. "You have always made me feel welcome, Orion," she said.

It humbled me. I knew it was a great confession. A weakness. Artemis was meant to have none. "I enjoy your company," I said in return.

She lifted her fine chin, indicating she'd heard me, if nothing else. "Would you hold my hand if I asked you to?"

I cleared my throat, taken by surprise. "Your hand? Will you promise not to turn me into a stag, and have me ripped apart by dogs?"

She looked at me. Clear eyed and unflinching. "Yes."

The day lit sky seemed to press down on my shoulders. But I took her cool hand and held it in mine. I remember her skin felt delicate and not like mortal skin at all. Like stroking the back of a lizard. No veins ran beneath her flesh. No wrinkles creased her, and no heartbeat pulsed in her dense flesh.

We watched the clouds drift as the sun arced overhead. She was silent. Unmoving. She didn't look at me, but she held her chin high and defiant.

I had touched gods before. She felt different. Eos had had rippled warm beneath my fingers, but the feel of her had faded with time. As had the slippery skin of sea scrubbed nereids.

But I remember Artemis, clearly, though all I ever touched of her was her hand, and only once.

Apollo came the very next day, as soon as the sun peeked above the mountains. I hunted boar in the forests that overlooked the calm sea, missing Sirius like I'd lost a leg. I hadn't seen Apollo in almost a decade and somehow I knew he would come.

"I heard your boast," Apollo said, his golden voice striking from behind me, startling the boars.

My prey fled into the forest and I breathed deep and turned to him. He was empty-faced beneath the glint of his gilded laurel. Nimble fingers played with his bow.

"My boast?" I asked him.

"I could kill every beast on this Earth," he said, repeating what I had told Artemis. "I am here to see if you speak the truth."

His listening in on our conversation riled me in a way I knew I shouldn't react to. It was bait. It was a challenge. It was the King, asking me to kill every beast on the island. He was setting me up for impossibility. I had learned that. I heard in his voice everything I had been too young to hear in the King's.

With one long, sun browned arm, he gestured to the sea. I looked.

The calm of the water shifted. The waves rolled and warped, sloshing up onto the sand. Something was rising. Something large and malevolent and dark, from the depths of the ocean floor.

My skin prickled. My dogs cowered, whimpering behind my knees.

Great pincers emerged from the sea first, and I stared in horrified awe. Then came the hump of a great chitinous back.

Then a bulbous tail, with a rosy-red stinger that drooled venom from a spike as long as my leg.

Water cascaded from the beast, in a hundred pale waterfalls. The creature seemed eyeless as it emerged, mouthless, and it had too many chittering, black-bristled legs.

A scorpion. It was as large as the temple where I'd sacrificed goats in Artemis' absence. The ugly creature's back was armoured plates of bronze, and its great segmented tail looped high as the trees. The scorpion blocked Apollo's morning sun, throwing me into stark, shadowed relief.

The sea will deliver your death, Apollo had prophesised. And there it was, death emerging.

The god's face was sweet and sour, pleasant and spiteful all at once. "Hunt and kill, little Orion."

"You cannot be serious," I snapped.

"You are the one who boasted you could hunt and kill any beast on Earth." His words were sharpened to a knife-edge. "So. Hunt. Kill."

"That is not of this Earth!"

"It is on the Earth now. So, great hunter, prove your salt. Or die."

When it moved, it chittered and clacked like a swarm. The trees by the shore bent and cracked, the sound of trunks falling echoing up the mountains. It was coming. For me.

"I refuse," I said, standing and backing away. "Artemis would not allow this; you cannot kill me here."

"If I cannot," he said as the scorpion crashed up from the shore. "Do you think a beast *from the sea* can't kill you?"

I erred. That thing could kill me. And as he foretold, the sea had delivered my death. I couldn't call for Artemis. She could never hear me during the day.

The scorpion was coming fast now, a behemoth, advancing up the mountains.

I wielded my bow. I nocked an arrow and shot; all one fluid, easy motion. The arrow flew, arcing towards the giant body, between the forward pinchers as big as boats, to where the eyes would and should be. A shot that would arch Artemis' fine brow in quiet appreciation.

The arrow bounced harmlessly off the monster's thick, chitinous shell, the way a drop of rain bounces off waxy myrtle leaves. The arrow fell to the dirt.

I looked to Apollo. He was glassy eyed and vacuous. He smiled a sweet smile that showed his glossy white teeth.

I ran.

The scorpion chased me for hours. We crashed through laurel groves, we shattered trees all up and down the White Mountains. The dogs fled. Apollo disappeared. I was alone.

I thought I could avoid the scorpion, but it hunted me. It pursued me. Relentless. I had never been hunted before. Even exhausted as I was, I realised the deep irony in that.

I climbed many mountains that day. And the scorpion was so large it could follow me anywhere. The creature somehow sensed when I neared a cave, and always managed to get between myself and the safety of a cave's entrance. It knew to prevent my escape. I wondered how much of that scorpion was a beast, and how much was Apollo himself. He would enjoy watching me struggle and fade.

And I struggled. And faded. My breath was gone by the time I climbed a cliff-face, thinking the thing might not follow me there, thinking I could hold off until nightfall. Until Artemis returned. It was only mid-afternoon and my fingers shook as I clung to the rock. My thighs tremored and ached. But even up the sheer rock face the scorpion followed, slowly, slamming its spiny legs into the stone and burying them deep.

As slow as it was, I was slower. The sound of its jaws chattering made my ears throb. It was hungry for me. Apollo's sun stayed high in the sky, lighting me stark against the grey rock.

I remember the moment I realised I would not make it until sundown. The scorpion, like a huge spider, worked its way towards me over the rock, and I hung there, so tired, like a snagged fly in a web. I looked beneath me, at the cool blue sea and then back to the scorpion. It moved inexorably closer, chittering and clacking. The cliff stretched up into the sky above me forever. I was too tired to reach the top. I could not stay and I could not escape in time, not before the scorpion got to me. My arms tremored. I glanced to the sea below again, blue and foaming. I could swim to the edge of the world, of course. I was Poseidon's son.

I swallowed. Closed my eyes. And dropped.

The briny water covered me, frothing over my sweated skin. For a moment I wondered if I could drown, if Apollo's prophecy had changed me, but I was buoyant as ever. I floated. My energy flooded through me, as soon as I touched the waves. Energized, I swam away, looking back to see the giant scorpion dropping into the water after me.

I swam further from the island. The scorpion was slower in the water. It couldn't swim. Instead, it crawled along the ocean floor towards me, tail swinging like a battle flag. It needed no air; it needed only me. But it could not leap from the floor and I swam far enough out that it could not reach me. Its tail disappeared beneath the surface. I could feel the giant thing pacing far below me, kicking up sand and grit in the water. But it couldn't reach me. I laughed; my lips and tongue crusted with salt.

And I floated. And I waited.

I waited until the sun painted the distant cliff face orange, and the clouds were pink tufts in the deepening blue of the sky. The stars above, Sirius as well, sparked alive in the dying light.

Artemis was right. Apollo could not kill me.

The sky dimmed.

I saw her then. Suddenly. A glowing, silver figure high on the cliff. Artemis. The sister moon. Relief weakened me. And then beside her, a figure glowing gold. Apollo. The brother sun.

Apollo pointed at me, far out in the horizon. He was laughing.

My relief shrivelled like a grape on the vine. It took only moments.

To realise Artemis could not see the giant scorpion on the ocean floor.

To understand Apollo had manoeuvred me far out to sea, and that Artemis feared ocean-creatures would come to devour me.

For Artemis to raise her bow and loose a silver-tipped arrow.

I watched it come. Flying in a graceful, shining arc. I imagined how many beasts I would share this last sight with. Thousands of deer and boar and goats. The last thing I would ever see. I didn't bother to swim. I didn't bother to even attempt to avoid it.

Artemis' arrows never miss.

I was not of my body when she dragged me back to shore. I floated above her. Above my pale, sagging corpse with her silver arrow pierced through my skull. She could not hear me. Apollo stood by, stupid with shock. Artemis wept. She wept and wept like she wanted to raise the ocean with her tears. Her grief was born, a living thing ripped from her body. Her brother stared at her shuddering form and backed slowly away, his face indecipherable. He won, but at a cost he was incapable of imagining.

Only Artemis was able to dispatch me. And Apollo had made her do just that, by first seeding the idea something was coming from the ocean to kill me, and then fanning her fear. And he did it for her, I suppose. In order to guard her seat on Olympus she could suffer no weakness. I was a weakness. And he rid her of it. He used the sea to deliver my death.

But Artemis never forgave him. It was never her and him against the world again.

Later, Artemis hurled that scorpion into the sky, changing it into a constellation. Scorpio. She did that for me, before she placed me, whatever was left of me, in the opposite end of the sky, with Sirius at my heel.

I look down at my hunter's hands. They are made of starstuff now. But still they twitch. Each night I am ready to hunt, I grip my night-bow and chase until rosy-fingered Eos unravels the sky. I never run out of arrows. My quiver remains always full. And when I light up the night; Artemis is with me. She creates the shadows in which I hunt.

I glimpse the beast even now, chittering and chitinous amongst the stars. Sirius barks behind me, ready to begin the hunt again. The scorpion chases me, and I him. We belong there. We revolve around the Earth. Around Artemis. Sirius and the scorpion and me. Onwards and over. We never tire. I can set the whole power of my being to the task without worry. There is never silence or death. There is only the joy of the hunt.

The endless chase.

About the Author:

Tee Linden is a writer living south of Sydney. She loves writing SFF, especially if it involves the Australian bush. You can find her tweeting under @teelinden or her website is teelinden.com.

FAIT ACCOMPLI

Barbara Smith

I am haunted by a slithering lover
who betrayed me,
leaving me to survive in isolation.

Whom once upon a headland
nourished me by cooling water,
drawn from blades of woodland grass.

The hunter within me is restless
while I roam the dark forests,
mountainsides and black water's edge,
waiting for the buds of spring to appear.

Suspended in this dark recess,
I have longed for my day of awakening
ready to transcend
into the Phoenix with a venomous tail.

BARBARA SMITH

Your subterfuge created a space in my mind
where the constant hunger for revenge
rages deep within

Waking hungry for a brand new dawn,
blood on my mind,
the power surges
coursing through my veins

The longing for revenge
is all consuming
My serpent tongue tastes the air as I rise.

The venereal fire inside,
dormant for many months, builds momentum,
invigorated by total desire to destroy.

It burns increasingly intense
dominating any hesitation.
The basilisk inside me will entice you closer,
allowing for the swift slice
to your throat.

Sweet malevolence
stripping the outer skin from your soul.

FAIT ACCOMPLI

The time is nigh.
Holding clawed hand on hilt
 I move closer
to the clearing where you stand before the lake.

My red piercing eyes watch you take elongated steps
enticing me to bow at your knee,
longing for my submission
and complete abandonment

I stagger but do not fall,
crying out— 'I am the God of all Gods'
plunging the dagger into your soft breast

Splintered light from a rising sun
highlights the spray of your gossamer hair across your
face,
wet from tears of dismay.

I wither,
as drought draws moisture from the vine,
languishing in emotional defeat.

Without restraint,

I thrust my death sting into my heart,

surrendering to my

'fait accompli'

About the Author:

Barbara has worked in teaching at Universities for many years and published her debut picture book, Otis Paul & Harry the Hairy Echidna, *in 2019. She is also a published Poet with poems included in the Zodiac series by the publisher Deadset Press.*

Having tried her hand at many things, from spinning wool to building an earth house, she now illustrates children's stories, writes in varied genres, and spends time with her beautiful family. You can read her collective poetry on her blog Lifeandbeyondblog@wordpress.com, where she adds some skills as a photographer. You can follow her on twitter @BarbAnn.

TRUTHSEEKER

Mikhaeyla Kopievsky

The sands are shifting. The sky overhead turns dark and the emboldened wind hurtles the grains at me like a thousand tiny spears. I pull my keffiyeh higher, the soft cotton covering my nose and bringing with it the lingering scent of cardamom and cinnamon. The scent of the Red Bazaar . . .

"You are too angry. Breathe." The old woman shook her head at me, gold chains and bangles rattling with the movement and sparkling in the amber light cast from the stall's lamps. Around us, the bazaar heaved with activity and noise. It was mid-afternoon, when the crowds avoided the peak of Elanon's summer heat. When the lethargy that had accumulated over hours of tiling roofs or carrying bricks evaporated in the cool air of the tented avenues and the chilled mint tea spiced with cardamom or whiskey. "If you cannot control your anger, you will never pass the test. And you will never find him."

With my head bent against the onslaught of the wind-turned-corporeal, I step forward, pushing against the maelstrom. My heart thunders in its cage, not from the violent weather, but from anticipation. *They will feel your anger,* the old woman had said, *and they will respond.*

I imagine them hiding in the sandstorm—the Aqrabuamelu, the Scorpion Men—with their broad chests, dark skin, and arms as thick as the fabled trees of Gaia. In my dreams, they had worn breastplates blacker than the sky at midnight, and their tails flashed ruby-red, glistening under the twin moons like blood on a scythe.

But it is too early for them; they will come at the third trial, and I haven't yet reached my first.

A different shimmering flashes at the horizon: not the scales of the Scorpion Men, but staccato flashes of white light. With each step, the sandstorm grows wilder, clawing at the bare skin of my wrists as I hide my face behind my arm and press forward. Even through the folds of my keffiyeh, I hear its screams, the wailing of a mother cradling a still and silent baby, the wailing that had exploded from my own chest just one year ago.

The silk trader had found me lying unconscious on the muddy banks of the Nera, my veins full of the poppy milk I had drunk from the silver cup of my wedding. His eyes had been drawn to my orange kaftan trailing in the water, "like the river had stolen the sunset from the sky." I sobbed when I woke in the back of his caravan, my heart breaking all over again and no prospect of death's embrace to end it.

"You are too young to die," he said, his eyes sparking in the night's campfire.

I was too young to be a lot of things; too young to be a wife, too young to be a widow, too young to be a mother, too young to lose a child. "Only death will save me from this misery."

He stared at me thoughtfully, kind eyes sparkling in the firelight, his dark skin turned bronze. "Death is one kind of truth," he said, "but it is not the only."

I drop to my knees and crawl, tucking my head into my chest and pushing my shoulder into the swirling sand. It is a sick irony that would see me die out here, alone and unmourned, after the trader had delivered me from this same fate back in Asana. I had been ready to die back then, but he had given me a lifeline—an impossible story about the Scorpion Men and their Sun God of Truth. I cling to it now as my body falters and collapses to the desert floor. I curl in on myself, shielding my face from the storm, feeling the sand drifts pile up against my stationary body. This desert will be my tomb if I don't move.

A mighty roar thunders from my chest and the sheets of sand swirling around me retreat and fall, the air no longer thick, the sky no longer dark. Less than five body lengths away floats a mirror twice my height and girth. It reflects my surroundings perfectly, but my own reflection is compromised.

"The Sun God of Truth will not be found easily," the old woman said, riffling through the crumpled notes I had given her. "You will first need to pass three trials, each growing in difficulty, each critical to making your way to the next." The money counted and stuffed into hidden pockets, she turned her scrutiny to me, frowning as she ran her gaze from my limp hair to my scrawny ankles. "You are not built for the warrior's test; you will suffer more."

"I have suffered more already."

She paused, cocked her head, and nodded. "The first trial will test your ability to know your true self. Truth has two faces, the one that looks outward and the one that looks in. You can not know the truth of the world until you first learn the truth of yourself."

The image in the mirror looks older than it should; dark circles around my eyes and a weariness that conspires with gravity to pull me down into the underworld. It remains still, even as I advance. I stare at my reflection as it looks down and away. It almost reminds me of my mother, the same stooped shoulders and worried frown that had followed me around as a child and aged her long before her second husband and fifth child arrived.

And then the image shimmers, weathered skin replaced with a youthful glow, the shuttered eyes now staring defiantly back at me. And just like the first reflection, this one is familiar. I remember her, the fearless goddess of my youth. The girl who free-dived from the Grand Arch Bridge into the icy Nera, who declined the honour to dance for the Vizaar at the harvest moon celebrations, and who fought off the winter wolves seduced by the plaintive cries of a hungry baby.

The sand ripples below the mirror as if twin snakes writhe just below the surface. And then the ground peels away, the sands coughing up two dull metal objects: a bronze stylus and a silver dagger.

"How do I pass the trials?" I asked, looking around the fortune teller's stall, searching amongst the silks and crystals for the kind of magical talisman that would guide me to the Sun God of Truth.

The woman slapped her hand down on the table. Smiling grimly, she plucked at her fine gold bracelet with a painted fingernail. "Each trial will confront you with something, and will give you a choice." The bracelet shimmers, tiny gold charms flashing in the light; hammers and scythes, papyrus stems, water jugs, rope knots. "Only choose one. Only touch one. Only use one. You can take whatever you want into the desert, but if you use anything other than what the trial presents to you, you will die."

Stylus or dagger. The options are as incomprehensible as the challenge—there is nothing to write on and nothing to stab. I step closer, eyes trained on the dagger. An accurate throw could shatter the mirror. But if I were to miss, would the trial be ended? I crouch down to reach for it; if fear of failure had ever mattered, I would never have stepped into the desert four days ago. My fingers are a moonbeam sliver away from the dagger's hilt when I pause and fall back on my haunches, the old woman's words rattling around in my memory. *The first trial will test your ability to know your true self.* Shattering a mirror of distorted reflections could be a repudiation of my false selves, but it wouldn't help me to accept my true self.

True self. I already know my true self—lost, empty, shattered. I am not weary like my mother was, nor vibrant like I used to be. I am alone. I am bereft. I am broken.

With trembling hands, I pick up the bronze stylus, its metal cool and heavy to the touch. I point it towards the sand, ready to write the words in the drifts. But the words are not enough, because I am not just broken, I am also a fighter. I pull up the sleeve of my kaftan, past the fine, white scar-lines of my previous death attempts, and drag the stylus across the pale flesh of my wrist. The instrument slices as easily into the skin as the dagger would have, carving out the Elanonian word for orphan, *YIHIXXYM.* The blood threads down my forearm, dripping from my elbow to sand. With the mirror still shimmering above, I stand on shaky legs. There are no more corrupted reflections, no fictions, just my true reflection.

I pull down my keffiyeh, and stare at the face that looks back at me. Wild-eyed and weary, but determined. I lift my arm, seeing the word carved into the skin transform in the reflection to its reverse. MYXXIHIY. Warrior.

The wound is a perfect paradox—neither descriptor true on their own, both true only when existing simultaneously.

The mirror shatters, sending tiny glass fragments raining down fire embers. Except these fragments don't scatter randomly: they fall in a perfect line that stretches toward the horizon.

The sand shimmers ahead, the impossible promise of water too much for my dehydrated mind to resist. My feet drag in the soft drifts, the resistance shredding already tired muscles. Death is stalking me and I am too slow to outrun it, and too sun-addled to outwit it.

"How will I know if I pass the trial?" I kept my voice low, worried that the fantasy of finding the Sun God would dissipate like the echoes of a dream if I spoke of it too loudly.

"You won't," the woman replied, pouring two short glasses of anais and mixing it with water to turn the alcohol milky, "until you find the next trial."

"But, what if I don't find the next trial?"

"Then you will die. Like so many others before you."

The illusion of water grows more insistent the closer I get. It's harder to rationalise away its rippling and reflection of the colourless sky, or its sweet, almost fragrant scent cutting through the dusty smell of barrenness. Harder still to hold firm the memory of the first trial, which slips further into the realms of a desperate fantasy.

"Desperate," the water whispers to me, the rippling on the surface growing stronger.

"Coward," it whispers again.

The water is shifting, the apparition morphing into three towering figures with translucent skin and amorphous features.

"You deserted your family," the first whispers, the voice a harsh gurgling as water falls in waves from the place where I imagine the mouth to be.

"I didn't desert them," I rasp, sinking to my knees as the delusion and exhaustion begin to overwhelm me. "I outgrew them."

"Liar," the middle spectre shouts, water spraying from its shimmering head and alighting on the burnt skin around my eyes. So real is the sensation, my hands fly up to touch the droplets, fingers coming away dry and warm instead.

"You abandoned them, and your duty," the third one booms. "You left them to avoid the weight of their expectations and dreams for you."

"Yes," I cry, the memory of their suffocating ambition too strong to deny.

"You were selfish and you were reckless," another bellows and I am not sure which; my eyes shut tight against the aberration and the memories. "You left the family that had sacrificed their own desires for your future, not for a greater purpose or a more noble cause, but for a flight of fancy."

It is impossible to not think of Richa. The same night I had fled from the harvest moon celebrations, I had run into the arms of my beloved Richa. A soldier in the Vizaar's army, he was handsome and brash and promised all the sorts of trouble and abandon I was searching for. We married three months later, just two days before he left for a far-off place and a foreign war. A wife one day, a widow less than a month later.

71

"You betrayed everyone for your desires and your sorrow," a gurgling voice calls. "You were selfish in your happiness and negligent in your grief. Turning them all away, turning inward, shutting yourself off behind your cold, dark walls."

"No," I whisper. Not everyone. My mother and father, yes. I had left them behind. And maybe I had broken their hearts— neither of them had spoken to me after I accepted Richa's proposal; hadn't seen me lay my wedding wreath or Richa's funeral wreath. Had never laid eyes on Arabella. Not that she had been alive long enough for them to have a change of heart, to forgive their daughter for the sake of their granddaughter.

My Arabella. The one I had never betrayed.

"Yes," one of the water sentinels counters, the sound of rushing floodwaters in the Nera. "Everyone."

"Not Arabella," I shout, opening my eyes to glare at the unnatural abominations.

"Especially her," the one closest to me rumbles, water cascading down its liquid body and turning the sand dark.

"I loved her!"

"You forgot her. Wrapped yourself up in your misery and melancholy. Her cries weren't as important as yours, her needs a chore."

"I saved her."

"You saved yourself from another loss."

The cruelty of the accusation steals the air from my lungs. How dare they? It wasn't true. It *couldn't* be true. And yet, the indignant rage that had course through my veins like fire just seconds ago fails to flare again.

She had been so tiny. A little caramel-coloured bundle of squirming and cooing innocence. I had swaddled her slowly, fingers drifting over perfect skin and fuzzy hair. I had loved her; I love her still. She had been a good baby, rarely crying, sleeping well through most of the night. And yet, there had been times when her little hands had curled towards my fingers and I had pulled away, too tired, too lonely to have any energy left to be present for someone else. Nights when her little cries had spilled from the wooden crib in our draughty room and I had pulled the thick woollen blankets up over my head and stayed cocooned in the heavy embrace of a non-judgemental, undemanding, comforting sleep.

It had been a still, snow-covered morning when I awoke too late. The weak sun was already casting soft shadows on the timber floor, the hearth's embers still glowing a warm orange, and the crib beside me was silent. The memory of Arabella, her once rosebud lips turned an icy blue, still flashes with cruel clarity. I had wailed at the sight of it, screamed until my voice gave out and my chest could no longer support the wracking tremors that pitched my body forward and trapped my heart in a vice.

I had wailed, but under the scrutiny of these desert apparitions, the grief in my memory is changing colour and shape. It is less pure, less noble. More selfish, more indulgent.

Tears fall from my cheeks to join the wet sand at my knees. "I failed her. I failed everyone."

Water rushes around me, soaking my kaftan and soothing tortured skin. One water sentinel remains, its form trembling and swaying in the still, hot air of the desert. "You have proved yourself capable of learning hard truths, but the real truth still evades you. The sting-tailed guardians will test you further. To know the full truth, you must prove that you want it."

My feet drag through the sand, pulling me toward the mountains that have started to dominate the horizon, but my eyes continue to track elsewhere, looking for signs of another pathway. A way out. In these rare moments of lucidity, I can tell that I am wandering wild-eyed, remember that my rations are gone, my canteen dry.

I blink and the mountains appear closer. I distantly wonder how much time has passed unremembered, half-lived. Blessedly, the sun has retreated behind dark clouds and the beginnings of a northerly trade wind pick up. I pull the keffiyeh from my face and lift my face to the breeze, closing my eyes and savouring this final reprieve.

The wind turns colder, causing me to shiver and open my eyes. The mountain towers before me, engulfing me in its shadow. On shaky legs, I take a step forward and then another. The ground rumbles, throwing me off balance and sending me crashing to the rocky ground. I brace myself for an avalanche of rocks to dispatch me, but the rumbling ceases.

Looking up, I catch the glint of red and gold plates, shining in light that stretches from four doorways that seem embedded in nothing but the desert air. I shield my face, squinting to bring the vision into focus.

Four men, broad-shouldered and thick chested, tower above me; their charcoal-ringed eyes regard me without curiosity or menace. Dark hair curls around their temples and falls to their armoured breastplates in thick braids cinched with bands of gold. They are beautiful. And terrifying.

The red, black and gold of their breastplates segue seamlessly into tessellated abdomens that curve under them in sleek, powerful lines. Four pairs of black, slender legs spring from each of them and end in wicked points that stab at the sand. They appear as statues, except for their tails, which glitter like the blades of a scythe behind them. Crowned with a red venom bulb and golden stinger, they flick around the Scorpion Men as though tasting the air.

"What do you desire?" The tallest Aqrabuamelu tilts his head at me. His voice is not the booming terror of the water sentinels, but rich and luxurious, like liquid amber or spiced honey.

"To see the Sun God of Truth," I reply, my voice rough and hoarse as I stand up.

The Scorpion Man's arm, broad and inked with henna, reaches out to open the door behind him a little wider. Through the opening I can make out the valleys of Asana, the afternoon sun a gentle benediction, its rays falling dappled to lush green fields and glinting off brooks that snake away from the Nera. "Why seek the Sun God, when you can step back into your life in Asana?"

"Or start a new one, here in Elanon," the one to his right croons. The door next to him opens wider, the view stretching out over Elanon's capital, to the vibrant city streets, the glass spire of the taj, and the canvas-covered Red Bazaar. People move about in that easy way of the contented and oblivious. I could get lost in that city, could let its bustling neighbourhoods and ever-present noise slough away my damaged life and tortured memories.

"Why choose a path you have already trodden?" a third asks, seduction dripping from his words. He pushes his own door wider; large swaths of green pasture and wildflowers stretch endlessly before me, a small village sits nestled in the shadow of a snow-capped mountain, and the brightly coloured ribbons from a maypole flutter on a breeze.

76

These Scorpion Men are not the monsters the trader or the fortune teller had made them out to be. They are stunning and seductive and offering me the choice of my desired futures with no payment but a few simple steps through a doorway. My tired body melts with relief, my parched throat swells painfully as I push down the unbidden sob of relief. They have released me from this perilous journey and saved me from the spoils of my reckless and hot-headed quest.

I turn to the final Scorpion Man, who has remained still and silent while his brothers have tempted me with their offerings. His eyes are brighter than the others, but he regards me with less interest. I peer past him to his doorway, but unlike the others, it is opened the tiniest of cracks. No light spills from the gap, his tail shrouded in shadow, its stinger appearing dull and colourless.

"What are you doing here, Kaeli?" Eron was surprised to see me in the Cynefin Clearing; he knew I should have been dancing for the Vizaar in the royal courtyard. He looked flushed in the orange glow of the fire, his hair messy and his uniform untucked. It was a well-known secret that the lower ranked Elanorian soldiers, excluded from the royal courtyard, were hosting their own celebrations that night; and I much preferred the haphazard abandon of roguish friends than the stuffy civility of Elanorian elite. I took the mug from his hands

before he could stop me and downed the bittersweet liquid in two gulps. My parents would be furious, but I would face their wrath tomorrow. For now, I just wanted to be free.

"You'll ruin your dress," Eron said, tugging at my emerald skirts. He looked handsome that night, unburdened from the responsibility that awaited him, older with the weight of what was to come, but not yet corrupted by it.

I knocked his hand away and handed back his mug, trailing my eyes across the raucous revelry. "Ruined dress, ruined woman."

He laughed, scoffing at the idea. Eron had known me as a child. We had grown up four houses apart, had shared the same wet nurse, had rumbled in the muddy banks of the Nera and nursed broken bones from falling off weakened branches in the Arto Forest. He knew I was no more ruined than the first fall of snow in winter.

"You look pretty tonight, Kaeli." His voice held a soft sincerity, floating on the bravado that liquor always delivered. I flicked him playfully on the ear and grinned. Eron had always been sweet on me, his glances and touches becoming more hesitant and less innocent in the two years since our adult rites. He grabbed my hand in his and pressed a gentle kiss on my palm.

For the briefest of moments, I considered what a life would be like with him; a good man, from a good family. A brave man, a gentle man. And then I had seen Richa—his bronze hair almost burnished in the firelight, the golden buttons of his uniform glowing like stars.

My hand disentangled from Eron's, my childhood beau forgotten. His lustre could never outshine Richa's.

"What future do you promise me?" I murmur to the final Aqrabuamelu.

He shakes his head, his braid rippling like a snake across his shoulder. "I promise no future," he says, his voice deep and resonant. "It is not mine to promise or pre-empt."

The other Scorpion Men are whispering to me, tempting me with the desires I hold tight in my heart and barely dare to entertain. And yet, I keep my gaze on this last guardian.

"To know the full truth, you must prove that you want it."

"Will you let me enter your doorway?" I ask, stepping forward to him. This close, I have to tilt my head up to meet his gaze.

His tail segments ripple as the sharp point of his stinger draws closer. I flinch but do not step back. "Truth is not something that is offered," he says, blue eyes flashing, the stinger scoring a line down my neck. "It must be sought."

My head swims, details once clear turn hazy and amorphous. The sharp lines of the dark doorway are fading. I stumble forward, my hands bracing against something smooth and hard. I push past it, searching for the heavy weight of the final door. I stumble again, slamming hard into an unseen obstacle, no longer able to discern anything from the darkness and silence that suffocate me.

"Why do you come to me?"

I blink against the soft, warm light that spills through the cavern and illuminates a thousand crystallised spears that hang from the ceiling and jut from the floor. A throne made of golden blades radiating like a halo sits upon a floating dais. I try to train my eyes on the being that sits upon it, but the light is too bright and I avert my gaze, staring down at the dirt floor.

"I come to seek the truth," I whisper, heart smashing against my ribcage, responding with the answer the fortune teller had made me remember.

"What truth do you seek?"

I think of Arabella, her tiny hands reaching for mine, and of Eron, his earnest eyes searching for the tiniest of hints his affection could be requited. I think of my parents, honest and hardworking, left heartbroken and cold. I had come here to demand why fate had taken so much away from me—to ask why I had been so cruelly robbed of a husband and a child and a life of beauty and joy. To sate the shame that grows like a canker in my chest.

"Was it my fault?" I whisper, to the Sun God, to the ghosts of my past.

"That is not the truth you seek."

No, it is not. Because I know it was my fault and because the question I really want to ask, the truth that I need to know, is *was I worthy of their love, even as I shunned it?*

"This is the way of truth," the Sun God says, their voice a molten river of lava. "It always makes itself known to those who seek it. It is never as hidden as we imagine, never far from our grasp. It does not take a journey through the desert to find it, but a journey to the root of the soul. You do not need me for your answer, you already know it."

About the Author:

Mikhaeyla Kopievsky is an Australian speculative fiction author who loves writing about complex and flawed characters in stories that explore identity, loyalty, betrayal, and rebellion. She is the author of the Divided Elements series, a dark dystopian trilogy set in a future Paris where identities are engineered and assigned. Her short stories have appeared in anthologies and longlisted for the EJ Brady Prize.

Born in Sydney, Mikhaeyla now lives in the Hunter Valley with her husband, son, two rescue dogs, four Australorp chooks, a hive of cantankerous bees, and the occasional herd of beautiful Black Angus steers.

Sign up to her newsletter to access exclusive content, early access to works in progress, and amazing giveaways. You can also follow her on bookbub to get alerts on book sales and new releases.

Find Mikhaeyla online at:

W: www.mikhaeylakopievsky.com
F: https://www.facebook.com/MikhaeylaKopievsky
T: https://twitter.com/MikhaeylaK

THE FLOODING OF ALICE SPRINGS

Georgia MacShane

On the 13th of July 1987, the main street of Alice Springs flooded. The water reached the steps of the local pub.

Connie watched from her window, high above the road. It must have rained throughout the night, only stopping at dawn. Polishing her glasses on the hem of her dress, Connie squinted through them. She didn't hear the rain, of course. Her Ma had always told her not to deal with water witches. She remembered the stories told late at night about fish-scaled sirens with impossibly long watery hair, illustrations in books that she snuck into bed and stared at under the covers. Connie hadn't done so in years though, water witches forgotten as tales to scare children.

Henry from next door swam across the road, kicking through the water until he reached the IGA. Connie spotted him, and waved.

Through the water ancient creatures swam; lionfish like monsters, their whiskers as thin as fishing line, and sea snakes speckled with glowing stars. Connie watched them all swim to the surface only to disappear again into the depths. She wished to scoop one up, seal it in a jar, to keep forever.

On the third day of the flood, the water witch appeared. Her skin was like smooth glass, and she had hair like waves crashing into sea foam. The books hadn't warned Connie just how the light reflected through her eyes, or that she would leave wet footsteps on the floorboards in her bedroom. She came to Connie and asked whether she liked what she had wished for.

"Thank you, but I only wanted a little bit of rain. My flowers weren't growin'." Connie said. She had never expected this wish to come true, let alone the witch visiting. She had never been this nervous but was fighting the urge step closer to the witch. Something about her drew Connie in.

"No one ever gets exactly what they wish for," replied the witch, her eyes sparkling as though it were a secret joke.

Connie pushed her glasses up her nose, unsure of what to say. "And the fish?"

The witch smiled down at her work. "A bonus."

Connie followed the witch's gaze to the creatures swimming below, nervous if she had paid an unknown price for them.

On the steps of the pub, small children sat with their feet in the water, never having seen so much in their short lives. They floated small boats made of folded-up newspaper.

Connie frowned, watching as the boats sailed along the street, until they sank below the water's surface. Swallowed by the lionfish, she assumed.

The water witch found Connie as fascinating as Connie did her. Connie's hair was thick and long, with wavy strands like crumpled silk. Her skin was brown as earth, and her eyes didn't sparkle like sun on water. They were more like opals.

Connie caught the water witch gazing at her, then turned to the water.

"Why don't you enjoy my water like the others?" asked the witch.

"Can't swim." Connie avoided her eyes.

"No one drowns in my waters."

Connie looked at the witch closer. If anything, she looked more like those sea sirens, the ones that drowned men and sung upon rocks. But those creatures didn't grant wishes, did they? "Why should I believe you?"

The witch smiled and her watery hair flickered between green and blue. "Why would I lie to such a lovely girl?"

Connie's eyes widened, at the unexpected compliment, and she couldn't find anything to say.

The water witch reached out to splash flecks of water at Connie's face, impossibly cold.

Connie couldn't help but flinch, hands shaking as she reached up and polished her glasses again.

"Come down," the witch purred, "have a swim." She passed Connie before stepping onto the window sill, diving into the water.

Connie rushed to the window as the witch disappeared. She leaned out but saw no trace of her in the water. The children still played with their boats, they didn't appear to have seen her at all.

Glasses in hand, Connie followed to the front steps of her home, the water just covering her toes. The children next door coaxed her, encouraging her to jump in. But the water seemed too deep, it wasn't what water should look like—there were too many shades of blue, and the fish were much bigger up close. Connie's Ma had told her to never trust a witch's water.

The sun beat mercilessly down on the town, making her skin prickle. Connie blinked, remembering she had forgotten to put her glasses back on. She did, and slowly the water doesn't seem that bad, the fish like little birds under the shallows. The witch's water still lingered on her lens. Connie wondered how cool and refreshing it would feel to escape into the water, and looked to her flowers in the front garden, drowned in their beds.

The witch stood in the middle of the road, water flowing from her hair, down her body and into the river. "Come Connie," the witch called softly. "Come and swim with me."

Connie smiled, despite her gut twisting in anxiety. The water looked so cooling, so inviting. Maybe she could go in— just for a bit. She stepped forward and dipped her foot into the water. A chill ran up her spine to the top of her skull. She gasped at the sudden, deep coldness. Around her feet, inquisitive fish came closer and nibbled at her toes.

The witch drew closer, her eyes firmly locked on Connie's, not letting her break free from her gaze.

Stepping further in, Connie moved as though possessed by the exhilarating water. The fine hairs on her skin standing up.

The children watched in silence; their boats staying by the shore. Henry walked out of the IGA, milk tucked under his arm. He called out to Connie as she slipped.

Connie staggered deeper into the water, arms flailing. The witch reached her in an instant, grabbing her hands, and stopping her from falling. Staring into the witch's eyes, shining like sunlight seen from beneath the waves. Connie's glasses slid down her nose, but she didn't notice.

The witch drew even nearer. Grinning, the water witch dragged her new love into the unknowable depths.

About the Author:

Georgia grew up in Wollongong and now writes in St Kilda, unable to live anywhere without the ocean nearby.
When not working as a publisher, she is either reading or neglecting a lot of half-baked projects. Her short stories and poems have been featured in magazines and online anthologies including Tertangla *and* Brain Drip. *She is currently working on her debut novel.*

She is online at:
I: @georgiamacshanewrites T: @georgiamacshane

DESERT VENOM

David Whitaker

Breaking through the stratosphere of Shaula IV and entering the troposphere, I've got us coming in sideways, one of our engines a screaming ball of fire.

"I pay you to fly, Micah, not crash!" Rani yells at me from his perch in the ship's command chair.

"You don't pay me at all," I grumble, cutting fuel from the compromised engine, firing up a couple of stabilisers to help compensate, and extending glide wings.

I hate my life. I mean, I should be on Vega Prime right now, burning my way across the circuit, gunning for the title belt, and living a life of luxury surrounded by race fans and beauty queens.

Instead, I'm stuck piloting this centuries-old rustbucket down to a backwater world, a mother of an ion storm licking at my tail and a bevy of malicious little nano-machines coursing through my veins.

Note to self: If you ever get out of this, don't accept drinks from shady-ass characters who *just want a minute of your time to discuss a business proposition'.* Planning to turn them down after they've said their piece, no matter what their pitch is, doesn't work so well when they've already hooked you with the first freaking sip.

"If I die, you die, Micah!" Rani, the controller of my murderous little nano-passengers reminds me, kicking his boot into the back of my flight seat.

"I know!"

Bastard little nanites with their stupid biometric feedback loop. Swear to God, they're the only thing stopping me from slamming a knife into Rani's toad-like face.

Without any fuel to supply it, the fire in our port engine sputters and dies. I pump some suppressant into it just to be safe, give it a second, and then spark it up again.

It roars back to life, giving me the thrust I need to right the ship and start pulling us out of our death-dive.

"Ooh, looks like Fly-boy's not all talk and glitter after all!" one of the Twins cackles from behind me, I'm not sure which—a pair of identical merc sisters, and two thirds of Rani's hired guns on our little adventure—the only way I can tell Eva and Ava apart is by the weapons they wield; one favours a bullpup submachine gun, the other a katana. I can't see either from my flight seat, and right now I've got more pressing concerns to deal with.

The ground looms ahead of us. We're still coming in far too steep.

In a last-ditch attempt to buy some time, I deploy the air brakes. We're way above their operational velocity threshold, but I figure I can get *maybe* five seconds or so out of them before they fail.

With a jolt and a shriek of rending metal, they're gone. The three seconds they lasted helped though—our angle of approach is a little less 'certain-death' and a little more just plain 'probable-death'. That, I can work with.

I scan the terrain ahead, searching for a decent place to put us down. Mostly, it's a lot of jagged, nasty looking rocks. Off to one side though, behind a couple of jutting peaks, is a glimpse of what could be sand.

Veering the ship-shaped crap-bucket toward it, I round the first peak, then bank hard in the opposite direction to try and avoid the second.

A grating crunch shakes the cabin as we make contact, but the lack of hull breach alarms indicate it's a glancing blow at best.

"What the hell, Micah! You *trying* to kill us?"

I ignore Rani, focusing on evening us out. He should count his blessings; any other pilot would have lost it in the ion storm.

Our angle still isn't great, but all things considered we're doing pretty well.

91

With the ground closing in fast an annoying auto-assist kicks in, deploying the landing gear. Killing the program, I retract them with a savage swipe.

"What are you *doing*?" Rani yells, kicking my flight seat again and again. "Deploy the landing gear, you psycho!"

"If I deploy it, it'll shred on impact and rip our guts out," I reply through gritted teeth. "If I leave it stowed, our belly is smooth and flat. At this speed, with soft ground, we've got a chance at a skid landing."

"A *skid landing*?" This sends Rani apoplectic, and his boot rams into my chair harder and faster. "You weren't hired for a *skid landing*!"

"I wasn't *hired* at all, you *kidnapped* me you slimy sonofuva—"

The Twins' manic laughter drowns us both out, and the sand rushes up to meet us.

As landings go, I've managed better.

That said, any landing you can walk away from, right?

The bucket held up surprisingly well; a few distorted stanchions in the superstructure, some misaligned power relays, and a handful of hull breaches. Most of that, I can fix. It won't be pretty—more like a cracked egg held together with tape and glue—but she'll be space-worthy.

"Good work, Fly-boy," one of the Twins purrs—Eva, based on her hip holster and ammo belt— "guess I don't get to kill you after all."

"You know if I'd failed, you'd be dead too, right?"

She just winks at me and disappears into the armoury.

"A thank you would be nice," I sigh, turning to Big John. "I mean, is that so hard?"

A cyborg four times larger than the biggest human I've ever met, and I'm guessing less than 5% still original human, Big John just scowls at me.

Too large to fit in the cockpit, Big John rode out our entire approach and landing in the cargo bay. Considering how close we came to dying—a bunch of times—in my opinion he was better off without a ringside seat.

The ship intercom crackles to life, and Rani's voice emerges tinny and shrill. "Everyone top-side, now."

I'm tempted to ignore him—the creep filled my body with a gang of poisonous remote terrorists, respecting him isn't high on my agenda—but Big John stands up and the look he gives me doesn't leave much room for argument.

We troop outside.

Rani stands on the peak of a dune at the front of the ship; a dune we created when the ship tobogganed across the sand. Eva's already with him, and as Big John and I approach her sister Ava joins them from the other side.

Big John isn't built for sand, and it takes a couple of failed attempts before we make it to the top; I could have left him behind and gone on ahead, but any excuse to inconvenience Rani fills me with a cheap sense of pleasure. Childish? Perhaps. Satisfying? Most definitely.

When we do make it to the peak, Rani and the Twins are gazing north.

"Yes?" I ask, making my voice as bored and petulant as I can muster.

"There," Rani smiles, his index finger twitching toward the horizon. "Thought you'd all like to catch your first glimpse of what we came here for."

I shield my eyes and gaze in the direction he's pointing.

I don't see it at first; its colouring is the same as the surrounding terrain, and its movement blends in with the heat shimmering on the horizon. Once I've spotted it though, it's hard to miss.

The crawler looks like a centipede; if centipedes were armour-plated, had a wicked spiking tail, and were the size of a mid-range shuttle. Its head twitches back and forth as it thunders across the sand, giant pincer-like mandibles flexing on either side of its mouth, row upon row of legs kicking up a colossal plume of dust.

"Yuck," I mutter. "You made me come all this way for *that?*"

"Like I told you back on Vega, that crawler's stinger is worth a couple million creds."

"And like I told you, I still don't get *why*."

Rani grins. "Because as you experienced first-hand, Shaula IV's not the easiest place to land, and ground up that stinger's a potent aphrodisiac."

The Twins burst into a fit of giggles and start making obscene gestures at me with their weapons.

"Sounds like bullshit to me," I reply, shaking my head.

"Who cares," Rani shrugs. "There are people who believe it, and they're willing to pay for it. So, we're here to get it for them. Supply and demand, my friend."

"Uh-huh. Well, good luck. That thing looks like a total pushover. I'm sure if you ask real nice, it'll just *supply* its stinger, no problem."

Rani lets out a snorting chuckle. "Oh Micah, you don't know how much fun this is going to be!"

Rani's plan is, in a word; *batshit.*

According to him, a crawler's back, sides, and legs are protected by thick plates of reinforced exoskeleton, but its underside is soft and vulnerable.

How do you get at the underside of a creature that scuttles along close to the ground?

Well, you mine the ground, of course.

But with desert stretching out for hundreds of kilometres in every direction, how do you get your quarry to move over the *exact* spot you've mined?

If you're Rani, you get two nut-jobs to ride out on performance-boosted hoverbikes with directional sonic emitters strapped to their sides, while a cyborg-turned-howitzer launches sonic torpedoes from the open hold of an aerial support craft. Crawlers aren't too fond of sonic waves, so if you get big enough jolts coming at their rear and a couple of guiding jolts hemming them in on either side, you can steer them wherever you want them to go.

The plan rates a solid 10 out of 10 on my own personal scale of sociopathic stupid shit.

For a start, I wouldn't trust either of the Twins with a soup spoon, let alone a souped-up hoverbike.

Next, handling the bucket while Big John flings warheads out of it courtesy of a railgun mounted in his arm is going to be a complete pig. I mean, it's not like the recoil just *disappears*; it has to *go* somewhere. And with Big John locking his feet to the cargo holds ground plates, that somewhere is the bucket.

I'm going to need to counter it, and you know what sucks about that?

If I attempt to counter too early, I throw off Big John's aim. If I counter too late, he'll *flip* us.

And you know what *really* sucks?

It's *impossible* to get the timing right, so I'm just going to have to be late every single time.

Recovering a craft that's been abruptly thrown keel over tit is super dangerous. It's also nauseating.

Neither of these 'minor' issues concern Rani, who'll be on his own hoverbike, directing the hunt from a safe distance.

I'd pray he crashes into a rock and snaps his neck, if it wouldn't also kill me in the process.

"Yee-haw, look at her go!" Ava whoops over the comm. "Like a baby cow gettin' her first taste of the whip."

The crawler, enraged and barrelling across the desert, its head rearing back and forth as it powers forward, looks *nothing* like a baby cow. I'm also pretty sure whips are *not* the go-to tool-of-choice for your standard cattle driver.

The Twins don't care, they're having the time of their lives.

". . . 'cause drovin's in my blood, and whiskey's in ma veins . . ." croons Eva over the same channel, hitting the chorus of her third or maybe fourth country classic since Big John launched the first torpedo. *". . . ain't no one gonna tell me what I can or cannot do, 'cause it ain't up to you . . ."*

Freaking junkies. The amount of stims they shot up before burning out of the bucket's hold on their bikes, it's a miracle they're still upright.

Meanwhile, I'm their eyes up in the sky, and I'm not sure how many more of Big John's special rolls I can take. As a racer I'm used to handling serious Gs, but they usually press at me from the front, not slam into me unexpectedly from the side.

Right on cue, three sharp pings rap out on the comm band. They're followed almost instantly by a colossal bang from the bucket's hold, and an uppercut of force that sends us spiralling.

"For the last time," I scream into the comm, fighting to regain control, "that's *not* a warning! Try a countdown or something, you metal bastard!"

The bucket careens sideways, our nose angling toward the desert as I gun the thrusters and attempt to level her back out.

Below us, there's a muted whoomph as the sonic warhead hits the desert floor. The shockwave of the blast is so strong my teeth vibrate in agony with the sand.

The crawler lets out a furious bellow and accelerates, pounding its dozens of legs.

"Go on go, beastie! Go!" Ava yelps, the comm filling with her laughter.

". . . and the town's they ain't built big enough, the girls they ain't built strong enough . . ."

98

"Rani?" I call, my eyes flying over the radar, the bucket clawing back into the sky. "Rani, where the hell are you? You're keeping up, right?"

It's not sudden sentimentality that has me in a cold sweat; it's the knowledge that if I stray too far from the slimy greaseball my nanites will lose their connection with his bio-reader and I'll be toast.

"Rani, you'd better be right behind us or I'm turning this heap around and coming for you."

"Micah, Micah," the comm crackles. "So hot-headed, so impulsive. Calm yourself, my friend, I'm here."

"Easy for you to say," I mutter. "You're not an active participant in this shit-show."

"Micah, you wound me! I'm the general of this grand endeavour, the leader of our band of merry men! Without me, what hope would the four of you have of pulling off this little escapade?" Rani asks, his voice weasel-rich. "Oh, and on that note. Contact in five, four, three, two, one . . . Mark."

There's a gigantic *bang*, and a deafening shriek of pain, as the crawler makes it to the mines and the explosives detonate beneath its face.

The blast throws rocks, sand, and dirt into the air, the thousands of tiny fragments cascading down onto the bucket's hull sound like rain.

Incredibly, the crawler doesn't even slow down. It just keeps tearing forward, its body surging through the swirl of smoke and debris. I'm not sure I can see any damage. If there is, it's negligible.

Ava whistles down the comm. "Wow, that exoskeleton is tough."

I sigh and shake my head. "Well, great job, *General*. So, are we done? Time to call it a day and get off this dust ball?"

"Call it a day?" Rani laughs. "Micah, why would we do that? This is just Round One. Girls, move on ahead and lay the second set of mines. Coordinates twenty-three point seven one seven two four seven by twenty-five point three seven one four four eight."

Ava acknowledges the command, Eva launches into a new country hit, and the pair tear off on their bikes toward the designated spot.

"You have got to be kidding me."

The crawler finally stops moving on Round 21.

We've chased it almost two thousand kilometres, hounding it over three days straight.

By the time it falls, it's lost one of the chitinous plates that borders its mouth, the opposing plate is badly cracked, and it's missing a number of its forward legs—some of the appendages are gone completely, while others have been severed at their joints, the mutilated limbs extending like jagged stumps.

In stark contrast, the back two-thirds of the creature's body is untouched—that was sort of the point though, and the reason Rani's been targeting our attacks at its head; he wants the crawler's stinger pristine.

The Twins cheer as it crashes to the sand.

Rani congratulates us, announcing how rich we'll all be.

I'm too exhausted to do much of anything. Days of recovering the bucket from Big John's rolls has taken everything I've had, and I've been puking since day one. I'm empty, utterly drained.

"Yo, Big John!" Ava calls across the comm. "Get out here! Let's take a picture with the kill before we snag our trophy!"

I set us down and the bucket rocks as the massive cyborg disembarks.

I don't even bother to unstrap myself from the flight seat. I'm too tired, and besides, it's not like they called for me. Instead I just watch through the cockpit glass as Big John joins Ava beside the crawler's head, and they both turn to face Eva who's fiddling with a camera.

Rani's still rambling over the comm about our upcoming payoff, lauding everyone but especially himself as Hunt Master extraordinaire. Eva lifts the camera.

The crawler raises its head, and the giant pincers on either side of its mouth slam down on Big John and Ava.

Ava's lucky Big John has augmented reflexes. The pincers are quick, but he's faster. Instead of slicing them clean in two, the deadly appendages are blocked by Big John's solid metal mitts.

Ava's luck doesn't last long though. As the cyborg strains against the crushing force of the pincers, there's nothing he can do to block the crawler's stinger as it flicks through the air and slams into Ava's face.

The crawler's stinger evolved over millennia to protect it against similarly monstrous-sized beasts—perhaps even to ward off larger creatures too. To them, it would land a nasty hit and inject a payload of deterring poison.

Against a human, it doesn't have quite the same effect. It doesn't even 'sting' Ava. It just turns her head into a cloud of blood, bone, and ragged flesh. Saying she's dead before her body hits the ground is a colossal understatement.

Big John howls.

I gun the bucket savagely back into the air, and can still hear Big John's ear-splitting cry of white noise and static feedback over the shriek of the engines. It's the first time I've heard a cyborg express emotional pain. It's also the first time I've heard Big John 'speak'.

He must have really cared for her.

It's not like he has time to grieve though, as the stinger is already jabbing his way.

Big John can't do much, pinned as he is, but he still manages to twist his body and angle a pincer into the stinger's path like a makeshift shield. The stinger glances off the armoured plate, but the crawler keeps pressing the attack.

Big John blocks again and again, the stinger's wicked tip missing him by mere inches each time. He can't do anything other than block though—it's taking all he's got just to keep the pincers from closing on him. He's fighting a losing battle, and the only real question is when he'll fall.

Eva provides the answer. Her camera dropped to the sand, she swings her submachine gun up to her hip and opens fire, a scream of fury intertwining with the stabbing rattle of her weapon.

The bullets do nothing to the crawler's formidable exoskeleton. They get the creature's attention though and it twists to face her, lifting Big John off the ground and placing him directly in her line of fire.

Eva either doesn't care or is too blinded by pain and rage to notice. Her rounds slam into the cyborg's back, shards of metal flying free as she unloads.

"Hold your fire, hold your fire!" Rani yells over the comm. "You'll hit the stinger!"

She doesn't listen, and by the look on her face the only thing that'll stop her is an empty magazine.

By the time her trigger does click on the spent clip, Big John's back is a shredded mess of ruptured metal and devastated electronics. The cyborg is missing a leg, and his right arm sparks at the shoulder.

Sapped of his strength, the crawler's pincers close on him with ease. Passing through his chest, they sever his shoulders and head from his torso.

Eva doesn't even register the cyborg's death. Slamming a new clip into the submachine gun, she unleashes another barrage.

The crawler angles its face away from her, shielding its vulnerable side.

It then raises its stinger and lances it toward the Twin.

Eva's submachine falls silent—and for a second I think she's dead too—but then the weapon spits back to life, raining bullets as Eva sprints across the sand.

The crawler strikes over and over with its stinger, but Eva keeps dodging. More lithe and acrobatic than Big John, she's a smaller target and harder to hit. It helps that she's whacked out of her skull on combat stims—she must have injected a veritable pharmacopeia of adrenals and psycho accelerants before loading the new magazine; every muscle in her body is tight and taut, her eyebrows are crawling up her forehead, and she's clamping her jaw so tight blood oozes from her gums.

She's a weaponised corpse—if by some freak of fate the crawler doesn't get her, her overclocked heart and brain will finish the job. I've seen it before, with desperate racers pushing too hard to snatch a win that's out of reach.

"Micah? Micah, can you hear me?"

I tear my attention away from Eva and pick out the approaching plume of sand from Rani's hover-bike. "Yeah? What is it?"

"Eva's not responding to orders anymore. She's useless to us now."

In the distance, Eva makes it to her own bike. She leaps on, fires it up, and accelerates in one fluid movement, barely avoiding the stinger which spears into the ground behind her. Throughout the manoeuvre her finger stays on the trigger, the air filled with the abrasive chatter of her submachine gun.

"Yeah, no shit. She's rage-blind and chem-drunk," I mutter, watching as Eva tears around the creature at random, bullets bouncing off armoured plates. "Only thing she's good for right now is as a distraction while we get out of here."

"Get out of here? Are you crazy?" Rani barks. "Do you know how much I've sunk into this? Sonic torpedoes and proton mines aren't cheap you know! No, no, we're getting what we came for."

I laugh. I can't help it. "Me? I'm crazy? What the hell do you expect us to do? Ava's gone, so's Big John, and Eva might as well be. As for you, beyond planning this cosmic cluster cloud of incompetence, you don't bring anything to the table."

"I brought you, didn't I?"

I raise an eyebrow. "Yeah, and I'm a *pilot*. Not a *merc*. Unless you want me to slam this ship into that thing, which I don't recommend, there's not a lot I can do."

"Micah, Micah, you sell yourself short," Rani replies, his voice taking on his familiar oiliness. "You're in a unique position, and you have everything you'll need up there with you."

I don't like where this is heading.

"Beneath my chair in the cockpit, you'll find a compartment. Inside is a little black box, and inside that is an industrial injector," he continues. "It's filled with nano-machines, very similar to the ones you're already so familiar with. These ones, however, have much simpler programming. All they know how to do is multiply and attack."

The sinking feeling in my stomach deepens.

"All *you* need to do is take them, program the auto-pilot, jump down onto the crawler and inject it. Then just let them get to work."

I shake my head. "Not a chance in hell."

"Well, you see that's the thing, my friend," Rani chuckles back over the comm. "Because it does come down to chance.

If you do this, there's a chance you live. Whereas if you don't, I will definitely kill you."

My forehead breaks into a cold sweat. "Kill me, and you're never getting off this planet."

"Oh Micah, now you know that's not true. You've only been through it once, but you're a good enough pilot to have worked it out; the ion storm that rages above Shaula IV only makes arrivals hard, what with the short recovery time, looming ground, spiky hills and all. Departures? Into the vast emptiness of space? Well, even I can handle that."

"For the record, I hate your guts."

Through the open shuttle door, the wind whips at my clothing like a hundred invisible hands trying to pull me out the hatch.

"Micah, is that really what you want to focus on right now?" Rani asks.

Beneath me, the crawler rears back and lunges forward, its front legs spearing the sand as it strikes at Eva.

She dodges the blow, just, her submachine gun a furious fountain of fire and screaming metal.

Her reactions are slower now, her body near its limit, her combat-stim overdose fast approaching. Eva's left thigh is soaked in blood, and she's lost a chunk of hair and flesh at the top-right of her skull courtesy of the crawler's glancing blows. She won't be feeling it though, the stims jacking her nervous system up into a nest of liquid fire that's far beyond registering pain.

"Honestly, yeah. Hating you is pretty much all that's going through my head at present," I say. "That, and the thought of this crawler chasing you down after I'm gone and stomping you into a smooth red paste."

"Very well. Though if it were me, I'd be working on my aim," Rani replies without a hint of animosity. "Remember, the injector doesn't have a chance against that armour plating. You'll need to go for the exposed area around its face. Eva may be distracting it, but your arrival on its back won't go unnoticed. Land as close to the head as possible to minimise the crawler's opportunity to throw you off."

Eva's submachine gun snaps out a burst of rounds that go wide.

The bucket's sitting so low over the crawler, it's in the line of fire. As the bullet stream glances off the hull I dive to the floor, the incoming rounds shredding across the open hatch above my head.

I scream profanities at Eva while the bullets ricochet around me, even though I know she's too far gone to register my abuse.

"Tick-tock, Micah," Rani calls, unconcerned by my near miss or the new holes decorating the bucket's airlock. "Tick-tock."

Biting back a snarl, I peek over the edge of the deck plates and try to get eyes on Eva; before I stand back up, I want to make damn sure it's not just in time for her to blow my head off.

She's off to my left, her bike kicking up a wave of sand as she cuts into a sudden tight turn, veering back toward the crawler, weapon blazing.

The crawler stabs toward her with a leg, blocking her approach. Eva swerves around the approaching threat–

–straight into the path of the stinger.

The crawler's feint has caught her completely off-guard, leaving her no time to react.

The bike collapses under the stinger's impact with a solid crunch, shards of metal and super-heated plasma jettisoning in all directions. Eva is thrown forward, soaring through the air like a ragdoll. She slams into the sand ahead of the crawler, a tumbling ball of limbs and dust.

It takes a solid beat before Eva lifts herself from the ground, and when she does I almost vomit.

Her left arm is broken, hand twisted at an unnatural angle, bones jutting through torn skin. Her right arm is mostly gone, the limb extending from her shoulder down to mid-bicep. She also has horrific burns across her face, chest and legs, the super-heated plasma having reduced her skin and flesh to the consistency of melted cheese.

The combat-stims are helping to stamp out the pain, but there's a limit to what even they can do. Eva's eyes are like saucers, her body's damage fighting through to her chem-soaked brain.

"Micah, with Eva down that's it, we're out of time. You need to go," Rani urges over the comm.

I tell my legs to stand, however they refuse to listen and I stay glued to the deck. I can't tear my eyes from Eva's wretched form on the sand below.

"Micah! Move, now!"

The crawler looms over Eva, its shadow falling across her like a black hole.

She looks up at it and raises her right arm, pointing with the tattered stump.

For a moment it looks almost like an act of camaraderie or respect, but then I realise she's just trying to shoot and hasn't registered the loss of her gun-hand yet.

The crawler's stinger slams down, hitting her in the chest and smashing her into the sand. What's left of Eva is nothing more than a wet heap.

"Micah! Go, or I'll kill you before the crawler has the chance!"

Rani's 'encouragement' isn't enough to unfreeze me. What does, however, is the crawler turning its head from Eva's corpse and glaring up at me.

I'm out the airlock door before I know it, my fight-or-flight response kicking in like a booster-jet.

The descent feels like it lasts minutes, though in reality can only be a couple seconds. The entire way down, I'm expecting the crawler to lance me out of the air with its stinger.

I land before it gets a chance however, my knees thudding onto its back, my hands scrabbling for purchase.

The crawler's exoskeleton, while tough, is also frustratingly smooth. As soon as I land I'm sliding, and if I hit the sand below us, I'm done. Game over.

I try to find a hand-hold, my fingers and toes desperately seeking out every crack our mines have created in the crawler's plates. Each crack buys me precious seconds, but the crawler's doing its best to shake me off. It bucks and writhes under me, denying me handholds again and again.

With just a few metres left before I'll hit the sand, my fingers snag a deep, ragged edge.

I'm not as close to the target site as I'd like, but the groove I've latched onto extends like a wicked tear straight to the crawler's missing facial plate.

My assumption that the crawler was a mindless, armour-plated killing machine was wrong. It's got more awareness of its circumstances than I'd thought, and unable to shake me loose it bellows in frustration and redoubles its efforts.

"Good job, my friend!" Rani calls. "Now just climb your way up and inject the nanites."

He says it like it's a walk in the park, and once again I want to drive a knife into his smug toad-face. The target site is about five metres away from me, but—with the crawler writhing hard to dislodge me—might as well be five hundred.

"You couldn't have loaded the nanites into a pistol?" I ask. "Or better yet, a rifle? Something we could have used to administer it from a distance?"

"Micah, do you know how expensive nanites are?" Rani replies, laughing. "What you've got there is worth more than all the proton mines we've used on this little adventure. You can't just load them into bullets like they grow on trees. What if you miss! I'm only letting you use this one because without it the whole job's a bust."

Shaking my head, I make a vow to whatever higher power will have me that the second Rani's nanite bastards out of my own bloodstream I'm going to take a blowtorch to his hide.

The crawler delivers a huge jolt, lurching me up and across. Seeing my opportunity, I take it.

Kicking off hard, I ride the momentum of the crawler's jerk and propel myself up and across, landing on the crawler's open wound.

The skin is much softer than the armour plates, and it gives under my hand. Grimacing, I find a new handhold—from what I'd rather not know—and jam the needle of the injector hard into the crawler's yielding flesh.

To my surprise, the creature stops moving instantly, stilling beneath me like a race-pod with its battery pulled. It then eases its body down onto the sand, as if it's deflating, and starts to sing.

It's impossible to put the crawler's song into words. The sensation can only be described as being dipped into a sea of memories.

Emotions and visions wash over me in gentle waves, each one a distinct collection of sights, sounds, and smells.

Closing my eyes I block out the crawler and the blazing sun, and I can almost grasp them. But they slip through my mind like forgotten flickers of dying flames, leaving me with impressions more than anything of substance.

I *sense* pheromones filling the air, stirred by endless movement beneath the sand, drifting through deep channels well-trodden and so very, very old.

Throughout the bedrock, cavernous cities spread like spiderwebs, criss-crossing and interweaving, the separate nests singing to one another in eternal harmony.

And high above the ion storm revels in its furious intensity, the power my ancient forefathers unleashed aeons past continuing to rage, maintaining the shield between us and the stars beyond.

"Micah? Hey, Micah!" Rani calls, his voice coming to me as if from across a sprawling plain. "You all right?"

I open my eyes with a start, mind reeling.

Rani's bike is parked beside the body of the crawler, Rani beside it and gazing up at me.

"Hmm? Uh, yeah. Yeah, I'm fine," I manage, pulling the injector from the crawler's flesh and hopping down onto the sand beside him. "Just . . . lost in thought, I guess."

Rani smiles and claps a hand on my shoulder. "First kill, my friend? Don't worry, they get easier every time. Soon you won't even notice, let alone stand there holding it for ten minutes."

"Really?" I'm not sure what surprises me more; that killing can get easier, or that I've lost track of so much time.

"Sure, the first one's always the toughest. Get a few under your belt though, it's just another part of your day," Rani nods, his hand lowering to my back and steering me toward the crawler's tail. "Now, let's take a look at our haul, shall we?"

I bob my head, my feet on autopilot as he shepherds me closer to the stinger.

"Good job, by the way," Rani continues. "I thought it had you for a second there, but you really pulled through. I knew you were the man for the job the second I hired you."

"You didn't hire me," I reply by rote. "You kidnapped me."

"Though next time, maybe set the ship's autopilot to land a little closer?" Rani continues, ignoring me. "We've got a serious walk ahead of us, thanks to yo—"

He cuts out in a strangled grunt, his hand rushing to his neck. As his fingers close around the empty injector—the injector that I removed still full from the crawler—his eyes widen in realisation.

He yanks the needle free and stares at me in disbelief. "Are you nuts? If I die, you die!"

"I know."

Beside us, the crawler pushes to its feet and shakes itself off. It then turns, encircling us.

Rani drops to his knees, veins bulging out across his face and hands. "Why?" he chokes out. "For this . . . this *thing*? It's just an animal, nothing more."

I place my hand on the crawler's side, recalling what it had shown me. "You didn't hear it, did you?" I ask. "You didn't see the cities? Glimpse the true nature of this world?"

Rani coughs, staining his lips with blood. "That? Who cares about that—it doesn't make any difference."

"You knew?"

"I've heard stories, drivel of telepathy and culture," he grunts, hands twitching as if electricity is firing through them. "But stories aren't worth shit."

"No." I nod. "They're priceless. Except instead of listening to them, all anyone's ever done on this world is hunt. And for what?"

Rani shakes his head, his body convulsing. "The prize is everything, Micah. You're a racer, you know that. You've felt it, I know you have. It's why I picked you," he gasps, collapsing into the sand. "But you're a fool . . . A fool that's doomed us both. And for what? Nothing . . . Nothing at all."

His eyes are already streaked with red, his skin grey. Blood trickles from his mouth, soaking into the sand.

I know when his heart stops. I know because my own chest tightens in response, and my skin begins to itch. Soon, my stomach feels as if it's being eaten from the inside. The sensation spreads from there into my lower intestines, and my lungs, then my brain.

"I guess you didn't really know me, or my nature," I manage, dropping to my knees. "You were too blinded by greed to see who I actually am."

The crawler moves closer—inadvertently crushing Rani's body as once I'd hoped it would—and twists itself into a spiral around me.

Lying into it I focus on the strongest images I have within me—every place I've been, every choice I've made, and everything I know of us and our place among the stars—and I try to sing.

About the Author:

David Whitaker is originally from the UK though has travelled around a bit and is now a proud citizen of Australia. He has a degree in Journalism, however decided that as he's always preferred making things up it should ultimately be a resource rather than a profession. His writing has found homes with, among others, Analog Science Fiction and Fact, Canadian Science Fiction Review, Helios Quarterly, and Andromeda Spaceways Magazine. Links to all of his works can be found at wordsbydavid.com

THE DESIRE OF SCORPINA

DJ Elton

Scorpina, the passionate young fae queen
walks through her purple court,
one curious eye on her beloved pageboy,
the other on the old king.
There are many days of October, but
this one is a confession day.
Or perhaps it is to be a killing day?

She is bound by ancient laws and must not
digress from her important role.
She must not choose her own destiny.
That is forbidden.
Let it all be left to the stars and the men
who watch them move, arrange and diminish.
She clutches a large white rose in her left gloved hand,
a peace-keeping prettiness for the old king
who sits watching her beauty, her dangerousness,
smiling self-assuredly on his old oak throne.

The old king adores his young wife,
yet he is not foolish or blinded by love.
Her mystique and attractions beguile him
although she keeps her secrets and obsessions from
him.

In his mage wisdom, the King
acknowledges her errors, understands her youth,
her erratic heart, the emotions she tries to conceal.
Out of love and loneliness,
he allows her to dally with the boy, tease him, flirt.
The king will reprimand the boy, diminish his ties
with her who is so refreshingly fierce and so so beloved.

She is the alchemist; takes in what comes to her,
finds ways to disguise her passion for the boy,
wanting to show the king she is authentic
as she wrestles with the demons of desire,
tries to quell her obsessions, do her duty right.
Out of love and sacrifice the king gives her help.
Out of love and duty, she reciprocates,
enabling her grand passions to wane and shrink as she
stops feeding the boy, although he is so beautiful and so
available.

About the Author:

DJ Elton is a writer of speculative short stories, poetry, and microfiction living in Melbourne, Australia. Her work has been published in several anthologies since she started writing seriously in May 2019. She wears a few hats; has worked in healthcare for quite some time, travels to India and South-East Asian countries, and has been a meditator for more than half her life, all of which add colour to her writing work.

RAY-GUN STING

Brianna Bullen

The scorpion should have been crying. Would have, had he
tear ducts. The flowers he clipped—snip, snip, petals falling like
a star—were tucked away with one claw and then two. One for
under the shadows of the roots. One for the scrapbook,
hidden behind the photo of a daisy-chain wrapped around
another Daisy.

Daisy was the cow who used to moo and move in the field
alongside him. His true companion. She had given him a name.
Scorpus. But he didn't like anybody but her using it. Daisy
would tease him. The Scorpion with No Name. Like something
out of a bad Western. Scorpus told her he'd let anybody they
encountered use his name if she would stop teasing him. He'd
stand beside her as she ate her red grass, while he was nibbling
on dust and a cricket, curled up safe and small within her
shadow. Her child. Born on a bloody September night when the
stars were filled with the scars of an electrical storm and
exploded ships stretched into string. Nobody could account for
a cow birthing a scorpion, but nobody was around to contest this

truth, either. In the end, nobody but Scorpus could account for Daisy's death. She had traded her life for his at a later date, taken by a grey alien dancing in the shadows, accompanied by the bleating of a trumpet. She had become stardust in the shape of her patches, because the alien shot before the scorpion drew. It should have been him.

They could communicate at night still, her ghost ever chatty. Mournful moos met chattering clicks. But when the sky was daylight dust, it was impossible. Thick purple bruises shifting on the sky's skin blocked their access to one another. There, he had only the cubes of light, the tree, and as of today the puppet corpse. The cubes held the tree suspended up in the air, blocking out the satellite dish sun and painting Scorpus' field below in shadow. The scorpion wasn't sure if the cubes were what moved the tree, or the tree moved the cube. A giant maple-oak hybrid, with burst-vein limbs. Its roots dripped blood and soil, some of the only rain and nutrients the dry but hardy field received, falling in the twelve-metre drop to reach him. If he had a tongue, he would have poked it out to taste the iron, but all he had was a stiff mouthpiece.

Scorpus burst the clouds that billowed through the sky like tumbleweeds, ray-gun fashioned from the curve of his tail. These clouds he shot were artificial baubles containing essential nutrients. A few bugs. Pieces of amber. The occasional lizard. They were all wrapped in gauze, the threads of a spider's web.

The arachnids of this planet hated him, but as he was armed with pincers and ray-gun, they allowed the occasional theft of their resources with only an occasional fight.

There were coffins in the field. Some open. Some damaged by time, bleached bone against sun. Others were covered tightly in moss. An open lid had spikes attached to the inside, to pin down whatever body fell in. The only thing dangling from those spikes was the hairy leg of a spider who had danced with death for the thrill of it and lived, sans leg, to tell the stupid tale.

Scorpus liked to shoot down the bauble clouds as they floated over the coffins, and hear the sound of his treasure crash against wood.

Scuttling over to a coffin to observe his spoils, his eight eyes caught sight of food in the tree above, wrapped between its limbs. A diver's parachute had snagged in the branches, the flimsy nylon torn up in the descent. The wires attached to the body still held firm and kept the soldier-alien suspended against the tree. A helmet with one-sided glass prevented the scorpion from making out a face. The body was partially hidden by its padding. Its primary arms dangled in the breeze, the right one snapped at an odd angle, held up by a tangle of wires. Snipping those wires would tear the limb from the body. Its secondary and tertiary arms were smaller, organised almost politely down the front like buttons on a vest—oh, Scorpus realised, they were only decorative. It was humanoid in shape.

125

He'd fought humans on his planet before, and had hidden from them often, the nosy bastards. But—due to having six legs—this was a different kind of humanoid.

Whatever it was, the alien would soon be metabolised by the tree. It was being pulled in slowly, minute by minute, to be absorbed by the many-mouthed bark, dropping fragments of blood and bone into the ground below.

The tree had made him and Daisy lazy. It had now made him despondent. Most aliens were killed before they even stepped foot on the surface, and he and Daisy knew how to avoid the creatures scuttling over the planet's surface. Daisy had been smart, and he had been quick with the trigger-tail. And now she was gone.

The scorpion stood, looking up with his many eyes at the figure held broken and unmoving in the tree. Cocking his head, he took in the blue blood splattered across the sunken chest of the humanoid, reflecting its patches against his scorpion eyes. A crying shame.

He was hungry for new meat.

Would the tree be mad and seek retribution if he tried to shoot the figure down? Surely it would still get an arm. Was he greedy for wanting more than a few bits of body dust by-product? He cocked the gun. Raised it lazily. If he aimed for particular wires, the body might just fall before he needed to recharge his gun. He had eight shots at a time before he'd need to recharge it overnight. One shot for each of his arms. But if he missed, the tree would think it was under attack and pull the body in quickly, and hold it close.

As the scorpion was lowering the gun, the alien in the tree gasped, its collapsed chest wrangling out a wet breath. It was returning to consciousness. Taking in the blood-soaked glass leaves around them, the chattering wooden teeth sampling their flesh, the alien began to panic. It tugged at the harness, finding the latch wouldn't open. The alien looked at its trapped and broken arm, and with its free arm, touched at the wire cutting into its flesh. From the frustrated scream, it didn't look like the alien was capable of regenerating its limbs. Poor thing.

Poor scorpion; if it managed to drop, he would have less to eat. Arms weren't as fatty as legs, but still had pretty good meat and flavour. A crying shame.

The humanoid struggled. The tree shifted and pulled the alien in closer. The struggling got even worse. So, not a smart creature. The brains wouldn't be that weighty. Another shame.

As it pressed a button on its inner sleeve, a blade emerged at its wrist, and it cut at the wires wrapped around its body and arms. This only tightened the pull on the wrapped arm. With a shudder, the alien stabbed at its shoulder, brutally hacking off its own limb, screaming in agony every time the blade hit home. The knife creaked against the bone, as if metal had hit metal, before tearing through sinew and out the other side. The tree branch holding the arm retracted, launching the limb into its main maw. Meanwhile, the alien remained in the tree, heaving. A wire still attached them to the caught parachute. No longer concentrating on getting their aching upper-body free, the alien took note of their dangling feet. The mighty fall. Their legs stilled before flailing wildly as the being tried to hold onto its remaining point of connection to the parachute for dear life with their single hand. This resulted in further panicked kicking as the tree started to retract the branch in closer to its centre.

The scorpion lined up its shot and took it.

A flash of purple light seared through the alien's wire. Grazed by the blast, the tree screamed. The alien flailed as it fell, trying to grapple with anything for purchase. They banged from branch to branch, like an elongated pinball, until they broke through canopy and hurtled down.

Scorpus tensed and adjusted itself, gun drawn and at the ready.

The humanoid was still, spread out on the ground like a flatpack. Then, surprisingly, it groaned. Blue blood arced out from its absent arm. The helmet had a crack in the visor, and a giant dent from where it had made contact with earth, but for having dropped over ten metres, the body had relatively maintained shape and wasn't pulverised.

The scorpion was relieved. He didn't like scrambled food, preferring weightier meat to liquid. Pincers out, gun at the ready, he scuttled over on his eight sturdy legs. The earth had now been cratered into a permanent body-shaped imprint. Maybe he'd be able to plant some seeds. Use it as a dugout against the giant blackhole-burrowing worms that occasionally wiggled through. When dinner was over, of course. He wished he knew how to properly store meat. This organism might last him a good six months.

The alien had raised itself up on its arm and was looking at him with a cocked head. Curious. Inquisitive. Like a stupid dog excited to be getting in the car unaware it was on its way to be neutered.

Daisy complained a lot about dogs. Planet-hopping spaceship hitch-hiker that she was, she met a lot of organisms and dogs were her most detested rivals. The scorpion had never met a dog. Had needed neutering explained to him. But the image of excited stupidity had stuck with him, and seemed to fit this air-dropping idiot.

"Aw oh my god, hey little guy!" The voice was automated, and yet sounded high pitched. Excitable. There was a slight rise in inflection at the end of the sentence that made the alien sound slightly ditzy. "Wow, thanks for saving me with your little wee laser gun like that. I owe you one. Oh, you're so fierce and all hissy and spitty, it's so adorable!" The alien picked itself up, legs snapping back into position with an oily creak. The remaining primary arm swivelled as if on a hinge until it was back in a relatively right humanoid position. The four smaller limbs running down its front all made a sound of being screwed back into place, before excitably chittering out. "I like your little patches! You look like a real cowboy," the alien swivel-sat right up and appeared to gaze down at him with a benevolent cock of the head.

Scorpus fired. It blasted right off accompanied by a ding. Scorpus scuttled back enraged, narrowly avoiding the shot which landed at its feet, searing the ground.

". . . That wasn't very nice." The alien crossed its one remaining primary arm over its chest in an 'I'm not mad, just incredibly disappointed' stance. "Although I guess my cowboy quip was a tad mean. I just can't believe it though. You have cow patches! I've never seen a wee little piebald scorpion before. It's very unique and you look very dapper."

Scorpus was completely perplexed. Took another shot. And then another. And then it was out of shots, trigger-tail locked and waiting recharge. He scuttled back.

"Very fierce." Their politeness was sincere but only mocked Scorpus. "Your aim is great! And your gun is super cool. I'm just a bit bulletproof, as you can see."

The scorpion stomped his feet, hissing and spitting up a storm. No meal for him, and annoying company.

The alien crept closer, hands raised and demeanour tentative. "Aye, no I am not going ta hurt you. I only wish to give ye a wee tickle under the chin and pat on the back. Ye give me dalmatian dog vibes and I wish to befriend ye."

Scorpus continued to scuttle backwards and almost tripped against a coffin.

"Living in a graveyard is no way to live, little buddy."

The scorpion kept his tail trailed on the alien. It did not know he was out of shots. He cringed, bracing for impact as the alien's large hand came down towards him, palm and shadow eclipsing his face. He expected death.

What he received was a pat on the head, soft and gentle and with the humanoid's index and pointer fingers. "That'll do, little buddy. Accept some kindness, even if it's from some weird, lonely robot."

The scorpion wasn't used to the odd sensation of being pet. At all. His tail reeled back as if to strike. A quick pistol whip containing poison. But it just froze as the lumpy fingers tickled at his head, rubbing just behind his eyes. After what felt like minutes, he melted into the touch. Not in a vaporised, liquified way, but in a leaning sense. He closed all his eyes and slumped.

"You wouldn't happen to have seen a cow around these parts, would ye? My cow's location tracker went cold here. Only reason I'm here at this dead-end danger planet. Looking for the hitch-hiking harlot."

The scorpion withdrew from his hand with a startle. Wrapped around himself. A clawed self-hug.

"You shot her?"

Scorpus shook his body. No.

"You know where she is though?" The alien tried to decipher him.

Scorpus full-claw shrugged. Pointed to the sky.

"She left again?"

The tiny scorpion shrugged. Made a slit motion at its throat.

"Oh. So I've had my cattle permanently rustled." The alien tied up its remaining sleeve tightly around its torn off arm. "My ship crashed, but I can hail another one. Do you want off this shithole? I could do with a partner."

Scorpus blinked. With every eye. That was an option? To go with Daisy's old partner into parts unknown?

The alien flicked out its fingers, catching a crumbling piece of his glove as it fell off. The metal of the finger guard looked like a thimble. Heat generated at his fingertips, melding the metal down. "Would ye like a crown or a cowboy hat? I'm thinking cowboy hat. Doubles as a helmet. Kind of." In his hand, the thimble had morphed into a malleable little hat. He put the hat on the scorpion's little head—well, his back really— and gave his right front claw a shake.

"Very dapper. Want to help me get some revenge for Daisy? Finally recognised that pattern. I'm sorry for ye mother's loss. What do you say?"

If the scorpion could have smiled, he would have. Instead, he scuttled up the alien's body and perched on his shoulder, putting his claw out in a gesture for a forward march.

This field wasn't big enough for the two of them.

About the Author:

Brianna Bullen is a Deakin University PhD creative writing candidate writing about memory in science fiction. She has had work published in journals including LiNQ, Aurealis, Voiceworks, Rabbit, Multiverse: An anthology of international science fiction poetry, and Woolf Pack Zine.

She won the 2017 Apollo Bay short story competition and placed second in the 2017 Newcastle Short story competition. Her manuscript was previously a finalist in the 2018 Subbed In Poetry Chapbook competition. In 2018, she was part of Nexus, an Arts Access Victoria collective for artists with mental health recovery lived experience.

EGO

B. A. Nielsen

Zeus sat on his throne, watching this new Age with interest. Below him stood the beautiful Artemis, her bow and arrow at the ready, focused on a deer.

But the creature gives way to another's strike.

"Forgive the intrusion, my lady," Orion said, revealing himself. "But there is no animal I cannot kill."

The earth opened up, at Zeus' command, bringing forth a giant scorpion.

Orion took aim, but the creature's tail struck him down.

Amused by the display, Zeus ascended Orion and the scorpion to the stars as one; serving as a reminder for mortals to remember their place.

B. A. NIELSEN

About the Author:

B. A. Nielsen is a fiction writer from N.S.W. Australia. She enjoys conversing with her two cats and eating Nutella with a spoon . . . just don't feed her after midnight!

SERKET'S CURSE

Alannah K. Pearson

The archaeologist squinted at the faded hieroglyphs, turning the smooth stone over in his hand, then frowned at the dishevelled young boy before him. "Where did you say you got this again?"

"You're the archaeologist Doctor Andrew Winslow of the shop signage above, aren't you, sir?" the boy asked, twisting his grimy cap in his hands, threatening to fray it further. "The gentleman told me to deliver it to Dr Winslow, said you'd know what to do with it. You are he, then sir? Will I still get my penny?"

"Hm?" he asked, glancing up at the sign above the lintel that needed painting again. It proclaimed the proprietors to be *Doctors Winslow and Blackwood: Consultant Archaeologists and Antiquarians.*

"The gentleman said if I brought you that artefact, you'd pay me a penny."

"Did he?" Andrew muttered but began rummaging in his trouser pockets for loose coins. "And the gentleman called this an artefact, did he? He specified me by name?"

The boy nodded; eyes focused on the penny before him.

"How strange," Andrew muttered, turning the stone over again, peering at it in better light. "Can you describe this gentleman to me?"

"Well," the boy began, trailing off with a meaningful glance at the penny still in Andrew's hand.

Sighing with exasperation, Andrew flicked the coin to the boy and retrieved a few coppers from his pocket, holding them back with a stiff nod for the boy to continue his account.

"This gentleman wasn't like any I'd ever seen in these streets before. He was all-over magic, sir and not like the tales of the Fair Folk Ma told me either. He was clothed in shadows with symbols painted on his flesh, far stranger than any I've seen on sailors at the docks, sir. He wore silver and gold jewels too, just like magicians in those tales you hear from Cairo? I'm a good Catholic and I was fearful he might command a flying carpet, have power over djinn and ghouls. So, I told him straight, but he only glared at me, said I'd best pray I never meet the likes of those who consort with the djinn."

"Really?" Andrew scoffed, checking the time on the fob-watch that hung from a long silver chain at his breast pocket.

138

"I'm surprised he knew about such men. Where did you meet this gentleman from Cairo?"

"I ain't never seen his like in Dublin before, sir. My ma always said curiosity be the death of me. I heard some strange language from the rear laneway behind Lloyds. That's the place sells curios and the like? In the big courtyard at the end, there's a coach-house but it was all-over shadow when I drew close. The gentleman from Cairo was talking to someone in that shadow, but I couldn't see no-one, sir. They'd been arguing but the gentleman from Cairo made me swear I'd deliver that artefact to you."

"You did well, lad. I'll chase down this swindler of antiquities and see him gone from Dublin's streets."

The lad nodded, scuffing the toe of his worn boot. "Can you read the writing on that stone, sir?"

"The writing is called hieroglyphics," Andrew said with a smile. "The ancient Egyptians used it to record everything from their trade ledgers, religion, and Royal decrees. Even though this stone is part of a much larger section, it's about the goddess Serket and the tomb of a young Pharaoh."

"The one with the cursed tomb?"

"Don't be alarmed, lad. There's no real curse," Andrew said.

"But people died, sir! What danger have I gotten myself into? A djinn would surely have been preferable."

"I doubt that," he muttered, flicking a second penny from his sleeve and onto his open palm.

"That's like magic!" the boy exclaimed.

"A good friend of mine is something of a magician, but that's the most he can teach me."

"The Antiquarian? Doctor Samuel Blackwood?"

"Why do you ask?" Andrew said, concerned.

"That shadowy thing at Lloyds spoke about the Dublin magician Samuel Blackwood. But the gentleman from Cairo made me swear I give you this artefact and not Doctor Blackwood. I was awful afraid, sir."

Andrew looked down at the fraudulent artefact in his hands and repressed a shiver. "I had best pay a prompt call on our mysterious gentleman from Cairo. Stay clear of Lloyds, lad."

Without another word, the boy disappeared into the swelling crowd, the boardwalks between shopfronts funneling pedestrians toward Dublin's market squares and produce vendors. Andrew squinted at his fob-watch again before turning on his heel, shoving the artefact deep into his greatcoat pocket.

Glancing back at the uninspiring shopfront he was blocking, he thought it likely his business partner Samuel would want the sign removed now. It had been a matter of contention anyway. Samuel was a more skilled Antiquarian than Andrew would ever be, but Samuel had cultivated a reputation as the iconic wealthy, bored gentleman. It was unfortunate that Samuel's reputation wasn't entirely a falsehood but to Andrew, he was business partner, life-long friend, and lover. He was also one of Dublin's most volatile scoundrels and, less well known, a skilled occultist and magician.

Bootheels echoing on the cobblestones, Andrew pushed aside a carved wooden door leading into a walled courtyard at the rear of the shop. Samuel sat in watery sunshine, a cigarette dangling from his lips, large leather-bound book open across one knee, a foot propped on the stone bench.

"The strangest thing just happened," Andrew proclaimed, searching his greatcoat pockets for the stone artefact.

"Do tell," Samuel drawled, raising an eyebrow, and turning another page in the book.

"A particularly stupid Curios dealer just delivered a fraudulent artefact to me," he said, brandishing the stone.

"Why you? You're not renowned as an Egyptologist," Samuel said, closing the massive book and moving to Andrew's side in a single movement.

"Your faith in me is astonishing," he muttered. "There's more to this than appears though. The courier was sworn to deliver it to me, and specifically, not you."

"That's worrying," Samuel said, translating the hieroglyphs over Andrew's shoulder. "Almost as worrying as these hieroglyphics."

141

"The hieroglyphics are fake, of course. But I planned to confront this swindler and I thought you might wish to join me in whatever capacity you prefer?"

"You are correct in thinking you've been targeted because of your association with me. You'll need my company for this, and not as Dublin's rakish bookseller either but as its only magician."

"Even my rudimentary skills in Egyptology can untangle the threat hidden in these hieroglyphs."

Samuel leaned closer to the artefact, resting his chin on Andrew's shoulder. "There's something much nastier I need to explain about this artefact. Do you know who the goddess Serket was?"

"That's a rather broad question," Andrew hazarded. "Which aspect of Serket were you considering?"

"Well, you'll know she was associated with embalmers and her scorpion aspect is often depicted without a stinger. That's poor comfort here I'm afraid. She was also honoured by poisoners and those seeking protection alike. This fraudulent inscription mentions the Pharaoh to get your attention. But there is a much less well known, more sinister story that when Osiris weighed your heart against a feather, if it was found heavier than Ma'at, Serket in her scorpion aspect became your torturer."

"This is all fascinating, Samuel, but please tell me what's actually worrying you."

"Serket's power over poisons is absolute as is her delivery of justice. There is a quiet following among certain magicians with a fondness for assassination."

Andrew stared without comprehension for a moment. Samuel had always hidden the truth of his role as Dublin's magician and Andrew had never pried but now, its reality was much darker than he'd anticipated. "And you think someone sent an assassin from Cairo after *me*? That's insane."

"It's not you that's threatening them," Samuel said, brushing his lips to Andrew's cheek. "It's your unfortunate choice in associates."

"Why send me such a blatant fake then?"

"To make certain you would take it. This 'artefact' you've been given is cursed, and not with a quick or painless death either."

"What? And how is my death supposed to send some sort of message to you?"

"Magicians don't enjoy the most balanced of minds," Samuel said, unsmiling.

"I see that. Well, we can't do nothing! What about the lad who delivered the artefact to me, will he be affected by this curse too?"

"I assure you I don't intend to do *nothing*. I am rather fond of you, Andrew," Samuel whispered, kissing his cheek again.

"The boy won't be harmed either. But right now, I need to know anything useful to track whoever sent this to you?"

"I can do a bit better than that actually. The lad was given the artefact at Lloyds and then told to deliver it directly to me. I don't have any proper details of whoever gave him the artefact, only a fanciful description of a cloaked man with strange tattoos wearing a lot of jewellery. The lad seemed to think he was some figure from *One Thousand and One Nights*. Exactly who *did* you provoke, Samuel?"

"I've always been honest with you, Andrew. I'm not an ordinary magician which is why I'm the only one in Dublin. And we are a territorial lot and those more powerful among us claim cities for our own, make alliances and form guilds. You're correct that this attack is not unexpected to me, but I assure you I wasn't the first to provide provocation. I approached the European guilds last year after noticing several cursed artefacts from Cairo had made their way into wealthy, prominent households in the British Empire. I've been expecting an attack from Cairo on my territory for several months now."

"You didn't feel it necessary to warn me I might be in danger?"

"Magicians adhere to a strict code of behaviour. But sending an assassin into my city to target you is a clear breach of that etiquette. The guilds in Cairo are among the most powerful magicians in the world but I am no weakling either. My response needs to be clear and without mercy: trespass on my territory, threaten those under my protection and suffer that same malevolent intent."

"Samuel," Andrew cautioned.

"You won't be threatened or harmed because of me."

Without waiting for a response, Samuel strode into the laneway beyond the courtyard, conjuring a small sphere of iridescent light above his right palm.

Hurrying, Andrew locked the carved door to their private courtyard and pocketed the key with an anxious glance to Samuel. He had never seen him so angry, jaw clenched as he nodded curtly in response and turned, coat sweeping about him.

They navigated through the narrow laneways that traversed Dublin, avoiding the main cobbled streets, but as they walked, the houses became more disreputable. Ahead of them, *Lloyd's Booksellers and Curios* loomed through the smog, straddling an unseen division between the reputable and disreputable areas of Dublin. Andrew saw a narrow laneway and courtyard beyond with a cluster of coach-houses behind Lloyds precisely as the lad had described.

Aside from confirming the name of Lloyds to Samuel, they had not spoken on the quick walk there. Now, standing in the smog and gathering mist of the eerie, empty streets, Andrew glanced to Samuel again. His friend and lover stood apart from him, gaze focused not on the crossroads where Lloyds squatted, but on the shadowy hulk of the buildings beyond. Squinting, Andrew realized the series of coach-houses had been converted into a single structure, far too large an establishment for this impoverished region of Dublin. There could be no purpose to such a large building, even the two-storey shop Llyod's occupied was marred by peeling paint, broken roof tiles and soot stains.

"Do you expect this magician from Cairo to be here?" Andrew asked.

Samuel nodded, adjusted his grip on the long walking cane he carried and gestured for Andrew to follow.

They walked swiftly down the narrow-cobbled lane leading to the row of converted coach-houses clustered together behind Lloyd's. Rage burned in Samuel's eyes and all appearance of the dashing, brilliant antiquarian Andrew knew so well had vanished. Now, the man was almost a stranger to him, one of the greatest magicians alive, challenged and bridling for a duel. He knew better than to argue with *this* Samuel. This Samuel could call lightning from a summer sky and burn Dublin to ashes around them if he so desired.

This close to the series of coach-houses, a single interior space uniting them all, Andrew could see how vast and sprawling the building was. "Tell me how I can help," he offered.

"Watch my back? I know you always do," Samuel chuckled, a flirtatious grin over his shoulder even as he stepped toward the building.

"I'm serious," Andrew hissed, glancing around them, the empty Dublin streets further silenced by the thickening fog.

"Stay safe," Samuel called back, stopping before the barred double doors.

Cursing, Andrew pulled the flintlock pistol from the greatcoat pocket and, with whispered prayer not to need it, hurried after Samuel.

Ahead, Samuel whispered under his breath, made a series of subtle movements of his right and left wrists, rotating his hands in opposite directions. A sudden tension choked the air as though Dublin waited; anticipation heavy in the atmosphere. Samuel flicked his fingertips and the sensation snapped like a taut bowstring. Acrid smoke and the tang of burning metal stung Andrew's nostrils and he half-turned to see the two large bronze locks fall sizzling from the doors. Cautiously, Samuel pushed them open with the toe of his boot.

Darkness yawned from the interior of the building. Samuel paused for a moment before turning away from the accessible entry and jogged back to Andrew with a defiant grin, a wildness overtaking him in a manner Andrew found unnerving. Without caution, Samuel embraced him, stooping to kiss him on the mouth, his breathing ragged with excitement.

"Are you mad?" Andrew hissed, checking their surroundings in case they had been observed.

"Quite possibly," he breathed, hands still resting on Andrew's hips. "Give me the artefact. Let them learn the consequences for threatening those I love."

"You aren't going to hurt anyone, are you?" Andrew asked, reaching for the artefact in his pocket.

"Of course, I'm going to bloody hurt him," Samuel snarled. "He was going to *kill* you, Andrew. Worse fates than that which had been devised for you I could not imagine."

"I can't condone death in my name."

"Your objection is noted." Samuel's rough fingers closed about Andrew's hand and the artefact. "He doesn't deserve your kindness."

"You're acting quite maniacal," Andrew resisted.

"I become agitated when the man I love is ordered to die," Samuel said, trembling with rage and fear. "Your death would have been indescribably evil, Andrew. Until that whoreson of a magician is banished from my city, the curse hangs over you like an axe ready to fall. You won't know it's coming and there's nothing I can do once it falls. Amongst magicians, knowledge of Serket's assassin cult has passed through generations. The curse delivered to you alone on that artefact is one of the greatest torments any poison can induce. It's a forbidden magic, Serket's Curse—as it is called—delivers a death of which no medicine or magic can dull the agony."

Andrew blanched with awareness of what Samuel was saying, was about to do, the certainty of the death he would be complicit in if Samuel proceeded. Any man who could knowingly inflict that evil on another was repellent. Andrew closed his eyes, unable to hand the artefact to Samuel, to enable him to murder another magician. He did not resist as Samuel wrapped his arms about him, holding him close for a long moment. Then stepping back, Samuel took the artefact from Andrew's loose fingertips, brushing his lips with his own in silent apology, acknowledging the pain and the difficult choices made. Then Samuel turned and walked toward the open double doors in front of him, the artefact held before him like a terrible offering. Unable to watch, Andrew turned to survey the vacant lane behind them, an inescapable feeling they were being observed.

At the threshold to the building, Samuel dropped to one knee and whispered a word over the artefact, pale blue light illuminating around the cursed stone. "Be ready," he cautioned to Andrew, but did not turn around.

Heeding the warning, Andrew turned the chamber on the double-barrel flintlock pistol, preparing to fire if necessary. Leaning against the stone wall of the building, he kept the laneway in sight and Samuel at the building doorway on his periphery.

"May you be welcomed by all the angels and demons of Hell, you bastard," Samuel shouted, kicking the cursed artefact in through the open doorway of the building as he released the same spell, he'd pulled tight around Dublin earlier.

Andrew watched the stone artefact slide into the shadows of the coach-house doorway, the soft blue light it had emitted extinguished as it was swallowed by the darkness. He shivered as the invisible barbs of Samuel's magic touched him and continued onward, searching for their intended target. The one who did not belong and was not under Samuel's protection. *The one who wanted me dead*, Andrew thought grimly, *the scorpion assassin.*

Rapid movement to Andrew's right caught his attention. He turned, pistol ready as a tall figure lurched from the mist, hands outstretched, the silver prongs of a curse on his fingertips. Without hesitation, Andrew fired, expelling the bullet from the chamber. The man stumbled forward, releasing the curse. At that exact moment, Andrew engaged the second barrel of his pistol and fired again. The man dropped, blood blossoming across his chest as Andrew staggered and fell, and darkness shattered outward in silver sparks and burning stone.

Dully conscious of hurried footsteps, Andrew stared up at the smouldering sky and turned his head towards Samuel.

"Not a bad shot," Samuel grinned, pushing loose hair from his face. "You avoided that curse he slung at you too. It's a pity about the wall behind you though, I had quite liked that fresco."

Frowning, Andrew looked at the broken stone edifice behind him, his own outline a silhouette against the scorched remnants of the fresco. To his left, a body lay twitching, blood still leaking from its mouth and eyes. A single bullet hole had cut a ragged path through the man; the second shot had gone wide, missing him entirely. The magician was dying, the rebounding of Serket's curse must have hit him as Andrew fired the second shot. But now blood and perspiration oozed from every pore, covering the man in a spreading red sheen as his veins bulged in a corded mass. His unfamiliar face was ashen, a contorted mask of agony as he stared at Samuel, lungs too filled with fluid to speak, lips too swollen to curse him. But Samuel did not take his eyes from the dying magician as he helped Andrew to his feet, dusting off the greatcoat and retrieving the pistol from the cobblestones.

Numbly, Andrew watched the dying man, this stranger who had delivered such an unthinkable torment to him but was now suffering the fate he had intended for another. He finally let Samuel lead him away from the destruction and his own guilty relief at escaping death. The only thing between him and that slow, leeching of life had been Samuel's greater power. Despite knowing Samuel was always much more than a dashing gentleman with a penchant for rare books and the occasional rake, his lover had never lied when confessing he was also one of the most feared magicians in the world. Now, staggering home beside Samuel, Andrew wondered if they had avoided Serket's Curse or if traces of the events today could linger only to poison them in the future. He felt Samuel's concerned gaze upon him and swore to himself never to let that happen.

About the Author:

Alannah K. Pearson is a speculative fiction author inspired by global folktales, mythology, folklore, archaeology, history, and the environment. Her short fiction features in anthologies from Black Hare Press, Deadset Press and CSFG Publishing. She is a keen nature and wildlife photographer, bookshop, and Museum devotee, and when not writing, she enjoys exploring the Australian wilderness always accompanied by dogs (canine assistants). In her other life, an academic background in archaeology and human evolution has her completing a PhD in primate evolution.

Alannah K. Pearson lives in Canberra, Australia. Follow her at www.alannahkpearson.com | Twitter & Facebook @alannahkpearson Instagram @alannahk.pearson

THE TANTANGARA CAVE

Stephen Herczeg

It was the nights that Adrian Cogburn found the worst. As the brochures said, western Tasmania was a nice place to visit, but after several months of spending every weekday and the odd weekend out in the wilds of the Franklin and Gordon river valley, he longed to leave and get back to his family in Sydney.

Adrian kept reminding himself that the current job was worth the money for such a short time frame. He'd been employed on a contract with the Western Tasmanian Hydro Corporation to survey a site in readiness for a dam that in five years' time would power Tasmania's newest hydro-electric plant. The last few weeks had seen the company move in drilling rigs to test the bedrock and surrounds. Adrian's part of the project was over.

They were making history, or so the Minister kept rabbiting on. With the completion of this project, Tasmania would be covered for its expected growth in energy needs well into the future. Earlier site surveys had identified the long wide curving stretch of the Gordon before it began its steep descent to the

STEPHEN HERCZEG

sea, as perfect for another dam and power station. In fact, construction in the area had first been proposed almost forty years before, but petitions and protests by environmental activists and local indigenous groups had swayed popular opinion against the proposal, sending it to the dustbin of time. Adrian understood that the chosen area had no such problems as there were no listed heritage sites affected.

Staring at the peaceful valley laid out before him, Adrian remembered reading about those past events. They were the beginning of the green movement in Australia. But times had changed, and the needs of the people had changed.

The dam Adrian and his team proposed would include the Gordon river area, just to the west of its confluence with the Franklin river. The resultant lake would be smaller than Lake Gordon, but it was the height of the hydro plant that was key. In electricity generation of this type, it was the speed at which the water could be unleashed that was the critical factor.

Adrian stared at his beer for a moment and contemplated the next few days. He wasn't due to depart Tasmania until the end of the week, but Danna and he were already planning a nice little overseas trip to celebrate. He had even thought about taking the rest of the year off to spend with his wife and their newborn son, something he hadn't done much since leaving the Navy. A nice idea and one he hoped would come to fruition, but in this business, he knew another contract would float past that

154

would prove too good to refuse and he'd be off again. Danna and he had an understanding that as long as the money still flowed, they were both happy for Adrian to spend time away.

Adrian smiled at his good fortune since leaving the Navy, running his hand across his beard, grown lusher than the normal five-day growth he kept it at, another hangover from his days onboard ship.

Staring across the vast expanse of Tasmanian wilderness, small niggle tore at his inner thoughts, the knowledge that most of this surrounding landscape would end up below the waterline. His eyes turned to an ancient wonder that had reared its head as a possible problem for the company. Down at the bottom of the gully lay the Tantangara Cave. A strange anomaly, it had never been regarded as a significant site, more of interest to geologists due to its unique rock formations. That was until recently when a local indigenous group lodged an injunction order with the courts. Adrian had heard that the matter was thrown out but had since been taken to the Supreme court. He didn't know much about it but waited to see what effect it had on the project as a whole.

From Adrian's perspective, he wanted to complete his job in the best way he could. It was up to the politicians and lobby groups to work out the legalities and moralities of the decisions they would make.

Adrian got to his feet and wound his way back to the path between the company's compound and the edge of the valley. Walking through the darkness, his thoughts strayed from the beauty of the night to the promise of nearby food.

A stick cracked in the darkness and brought him up short. Confused, Adrian peered into the gloom. There weren't any animals large enough to make that kind of noise in the area. The site manager had mentioned a local population of devils, but those marsupials would run as soon as they saw or heard a human.

Another stick cracked. From the gloom came the unmistakable sound of footsteps coming towards him.

"Hey, who's there?"

The footsteps stopped, but there was no reply. He waited for a moment, then shrugged and continued on into the dark.

Adrian turned as another loud crack echoed out behind him. Staring into the darkness; he was almost sure he could make out movement in the pitch black. "Okay, you bastards, this isn't funny. I know I'm leaving soon, but you can keep your stupid pranks to yourself."

The shape remained silent, but dim light reflected off a shiny surface.

Confused, Adrian stepped forward, hoping to get a better look. "Come on, I just want to get back to camp and eat, it's getting late." He stared at the dark shape, transfixed by the movement of reflected light as it swayed from side to side. Sudden anger welled inside at the audacity of a colleague to play such a stupid joke on him. Taking two steps forward, he raised the beer bottle in his hand. "Right, that's it, whoever you are, I've had enough."

Something dark and shiny darted from the gloom and disappeared just as fast. The bottle dropped from Adrian's hand, smashing on a protruding rock. A stab of sharp pain spread across his chest, followed by a growing and contrasting sense of numbness.

Adrian glanced down. A small line of blood dribble down his shirt. He tried to touch the wound, but his fingers were like icicles. Bringing one hand up to his face, the dark blood staining his fingers was visible, but there was no warm wetness.

Trying to distinguish the form of his attacker in the surrounding gloom, Adrian's mind grew vague and fuzzy, as if his head was full of cotton wool. He staggered forward, his legs losing strength and feeling, before crashing to his knees. Dark spots clouded his sight and he fell face-first into the dirt.

A noise echoed from the darkness; a clacking followed by the *crunching* of dried sticks as something large moved away from its victim.

"The Gordon Valley hydro-electric power station will be the most important addition to Tasmania's energy mix in the twenty-first century." The Tasmanian Minister of Energy stood proud on the podium, a natural showman on stage before a captive audience. Flanking him, several men in suits and a group of local council members nodded agreement to every word.

From behind the crush of reporters and observers straining to hear what the Minister said, Col Colbert scanned the crowd for any potential trouble. He didn't care two hoots about the message the Minister was selling, he was a reporter and could smell a potential flare-up.

"To show our commitment to the town of Strathgordon and the surrounding area, the Tasmanian Government has built this council chamber," continued the Minister, gesturing around the room, "and the local hospital. We want Strathgordon to become a hub of industry for both central and western Tasmania."

A nagging question rose in Colbert's mind. He glanced around the room, confused when he remembered the construction for this place was finalised over a year ago.

Does that mean the dam project has been in motion for years?

As the question-and-answer session began, Colbert's hopes rose of something worth reporting on. Hands shot up from reporters across the room, straining for a chance to ask one of several scripted questions. Colbert was a little ashamed by his fellow reporters, everything they asked was in the glossy brochures provided at the entrance to the town hall or could be found on the Ministry's website. The Minister passed the torch to another middle-aged man in a dark suit, Novak Sujdovic, Chief Executive Officer of the Western Tasmanian Hydro Corporation.

"What about the cultural destruction of sacred aboriginal heritage sites?" asked the familiar voice of Freddie Fisk, a reporter who was of a similar age and level of cynicism as Colbert himself.

Colbert expected the Minister to grow pale and withdraw from the room as the question was made verbal. To his surprise, the Minister smiled calmly and waited for the din to die down before replying in a smooth, well-rehearsed way. "We have consulted the best archaeologists in Tasmania and indeed, the rest of Australia. The consensus is that the cave in question has never known human occupation, and indeed does not feature in any of the legends or stories of the local indigenous population. The local court has declared that the injunction order was lodged was a nuisance to delay the project. I'm sure the Supreme Court will rule in much the same way soon. The only people concerned about the significance of the Tantangara Cave are a group of activists bent on halting the progress of the Tasmanian people."

"That's bullshit!" Someone cried from the back of the crowd.

"Ah, there's one of them now," said the Minister.

Colbert swung his phone around, capturing an image of the speaker. She had dark brown skin and deep black hair that fell in tight ringlets. Colbert didn't know who this woman was but made sure to get a good image for later investigation.

"You paid off the courts! The company paid them off! They are selling out our lands and our heritage."

Noticing the Minister move to one side, Colbert watched him lean towards a nearby aid, who signaled the Security Guards standing at the back of the hall.

"Yes, Miss Tanner, you've had quite a lot to say about this matter, but please respect the rest of us and leave," said the Minister.

As the agitator, Miss Tanner, was whisked from the room, her language turned into a verbal tirade directed at all members of the thieving white race and their sycophants.

All eyes turned back to the smiling visage of the Minister. "If there are no more questions, then," the Minister said before turning to leave.

Before any of the reporters could even raise their hands, he left the stage. Colbert pretended to check the video on his phone but kept an eye on the group at the front. They were hustled through a back door by a well-dressed man in a suit, who Colbert figured was another bureaucrat or aide for the Minister.

Waiting until the remaining people had wandered from the audience room, leaving only himself and a lone security guard, Colbert sidled up to the back door used by the Minister.

"Oi, what are you doing?" the guard shouted.

Colbert pulled out his journalist licence and showed it to the guard. "I've got an interview with the Minister. It's just through here, right?"

The guard eyed him suspiciously then took a longer look at the licence before nodding. "All right, but I thought you guys were meant to go through the main entrance?"

"I was told to wait until after the news conference but couldn't follow the Minister straight away. There was a crush of people."

Thinking for a long time again, the guard nodded, grabbed the doorknob, opening it enough to allow Colbert through.

Stepping into an empty corridor, Colbert feigned enough confidence to ensure the guard would believe he knew where he was and what he was doing, and strode down the corridor. Breathing a sigh of relief, Colbert listened for any indication of where the Minister and his coterie might have gone.

Voices drifted from further down the adjoining passage, attracting his attention. Colbert realised they were approaching, and ducked through an open doorway, pressing his shoulder to

161

the door frame and listening for any useful conversation. He pulled out his phone and switched on the recording function.

In the corridor beyond, two men walked together deep in conversation. Colbert could make out only fragments and hoped the phone was picking up the rest.

"He was found not far from the campsite."

"Away from the cave?"

"Yes, on a ridge overlooking the valley."

"Good, good. Well, not good, but you know. Stabbed you said? Do we know who?"

"One of the engineers. He'd finished up and was leaving tomorrow."

"Was he an arsehole or something? Picked a fight? These men can get violent when they get on the piss."

"Nobody's owning up. Most say he was quiet, an unassuming guy. Kept to himself."

"Bugger. Are the cops involved yet?"

"Yeah. They want to talk to you."

"This could delay things. Not good. The Minister will be pissed off. The Board will have my guts."

"The police have cordoned off the area, but the rest of the operation is free. They said they want to conduct interviews, shouldn't take too long."

"Good. And the body?"

"It's at the hospital. The police ordered an autopsy."

"The press?"

"We've managed to keep a lid on it so far, but who knows. Our people know how to keep quiet, but we can't stop the police from talking."

"Play along with anything they want. If we shut up shop that's when the police will start talking. And keep me informed of everything? We're running behind schedule as it is with all these stupid activists getting in the way."

"Yes, Sir."

The younger of the two men turned around, back the way they had come and disappeared. The other man turned towards Colbert and he realised it was Sujdovic, the CEO of the Hydro company. Withdrawing further into the gloom of the darkened room, Colbert waited as the man pulled out a phone and dialled.

"Gianni, what the hell's happening out there?"

Colbert could just hear the response and cursed under his breath.

"This has nothing to do with Tanner and her mob does it?" Sujdovic asked, and as he listened to the reply, his grimace relaxed. "Good then. She was here today. I wanted to make sure they aren't ramping things up at your end? I've got Smithers to keep on top of it here, so just keep me informed if anything else happens, okay?"

Sujdovic listened to the voice on the other end and then hung up, putting his phone away. Assuming he was alone, he let out an exasperated breath. "Why the fuck now?" he swore, before stomping off down the hall.

In the shadows, Colbert smiled to himself, turning his phone over and tapped the *stop* icon. He tapped *play* and held it to his ear, smile widening as the conversation replayed with high clarity.

"You'll turn that lobster into a pineapple, and I might just let you have a look."

Selma Balletto reached for the fifty dollar note as Colbert pulled it out of his wallet. Smiling, she folded and slipped it into a pocket beneath her pristine white lab coat.

"What are you a vegetarian or something?" He asked.

"No, but a girl's gotta eat. It's either cold hard cash or you could take me out for dinner," she said with a cheeky smile before glancing to check they were alone. Then, Selma opened the morgue doors and led him to a gurney holding a body, draped in the obligatory white sheet. Reaching for the edges of the starched white material, she asked, "You sure you wanna look at this?"

"I just paid fifty bucks for a viewing, damn straight I do." Colbert said, holding his phone out already, video recorder running.

Selma pulled the sheet away and Colbert gave a small but involuntary gasp. Adrian Cogburn's body wasn't what he had expected to see.

"What the hell did that?" Colbert asked.

The engineer's skin was tinged a slight blue, as if he had been suffocated rather than stabbed. A distinct circular hole was exposed in the middle of his chest, it edges well-formed and showing a definite dark bruising pattern.

Pointing towards the hole, Selma's voice adopted a professional tone, as if this were her official coronial record for Colbert's cause of death. "As you can see, the victim received a circular puncture wound to the chest. The blow was delivered with a needle-like weapon, puncturing deep into the heart and leading me to surmise that the victim died almost immediately." She hesitated and then stopped.

"But?"

"Yes, but he didn't," she continued. "The discolouration to his skin suggests the presence of some type of toxin."

"He was poisoned?"

Selma nodded and continued. "I'm still waiting on the toxicology report, but the skin colour suggests he was still alive for at least several minutes after the attack."

"Why?"

"Well, his heart was still pumping, but his lungs were no longer drawing air. So, deoxygenated blood was being pumped around his body. That can happen due to certain types of neurotoxins. It occurs often with small animals and insects that have been injected."

"I'm lost."

"Oh, sorry. When you're living out here you need to know the local predator species to ensure that humans can be treated. The forests of this area are safe. There's nothing very dangerous around here, apart from devils."

"No snakes or spiders?"

"There are three slightly venomous species of snake, and of course we have redbacks and funnel webs."

"But none of them did this?"

"I doubt it. The size of the puncture wound is massive compared to the tiny fangs of a snake or spider, plus the amount of venom required would be huge."

"I had assumed he was killed by a work mate because of a fight or something."

Selma shrugged and pulled the sheet back to cover Adrian's body. "Maybe? It's possible the assailant had an ice-pick or something, or maybe a piece of machinery. That could account for the puncture wound," she said, shaking her head. "But if there's any poison or venom to be found, I've got no idea how it was delivered at this stage."

Colbert switched off his recorder and stared at the covered corpse on the gurney for a moment. A nagging instinct in the back of his mind insisted there was an interesting story here, but more digging was required before he could even start to write.

Her footsteps crunching on the gravel and broken stones that littered the floor, Karrie Silend moved deeper into the cave. The walk down into the valley had been exhilarating, but the load of equipment in her arms had brought out a light sheen of sweat across her exposed skin and shortening of breath as she gasped slightly with the effort.

Placing her belongings on the ground, Karrie picked up a small battery powered light on a tripod and turned it on, illuminating the immediate area. She smiled at the sight before her. The cave was spectacular. Her mood diminished though with the realisation why she was there. The boss had wanted the cave photographed and mapped out, so the engineers back on the mainland could study it and advise on the best placement of the mine entrance, from both an efficiency and clandestine perspective. Karrie hadn't agreed to the idea of mining into the surrounding area, and part of her was angry at using the Tantangara cave as a disguised entrance to the mine.

But ain't nobody else paying me as much, so suck it up.

Depositing her backpack to the ground, Karrie pulled out a handful of glow sticks, and her camera. She stepped beyond the work light and started to take photos of the area. After confirming the GPS indicator on the camera was working, she continued to fire off several photos before moving further into the cave system.

Within moments she was in relative darkness, well out of the range from the lone work light. Switching on her helmet mounted torch, she checked the camera once more, turning up the ISO factor to accommodate the lack of ambient light, and continued deeper into the cave network, the muted clicks from the digital camera echoed through the darkened maze around her.

After several minutes, Karrie stopped again to take a breather. Sucking in a breath, she couldn't help but notice the damp feel and dirty taste to the air. Letting her camera hang by its strap, she took a long drink from her canteen, and shivered when she realised how cold it had become. Glancing around, she could discern the already dimming light from the glowsticks, and the yellow shine they gave the immediate area.

A *crunch*, followed by the rattle of pebbles sliding down a slope, echoed from the bowels of the dark cave ahead. Another shiver ran down her spine, and Karrie was unsure if it was from the sound or just the cold.

Should have brought Gianni with me. This part of the cave always gives me the creeps.

Shrugging, she replaced the canteen into her bag and picked up her camera. Stepping forward and clicking away.

The sudden flash almost blinded her as each successive burst of dazzling white light seemed brighter than the first. There was another *crunch* that echoed from nearby. Karrie turned in that direction, using her camera to fire off several shots. The blinding afterimage made her sure she saw the movement in the dark. Holding the camera away from her, she kept shooting and staring into the gloom, trying to identify anything out of place.

Several *scraping* noises carried towards her. She fired the camera flash, light reflecting and refracting off something large, dark, and shiny as it moved around the cavern. Sucking in a breath, Karrie's eyes suddenly grew wide in fear.

Something's there. In here with me.

Turning, Karrie tried to track the movement and kept the camera flashing. She cried out in pain as something grabbed her around the stomach and squeezed.

Bringing the camera up, she depressed the shutter release button, the flash reflected off two dozen dark orbs before her. A high-pitched squeal echoed from the dark, the pain intensifying as she was crushed tighter. Another flare burned into the afterimage of something long and sharp that hovered above those orbs. Almost in reflex, her finger depressed the button again, and the final flash revealed the source of the movement.

Pain erupted through Karrie's chest. She let out a single, surprised scream before the darkness claimed her.

Pulling his zippo lighter from his pocket, Colbert lit the cigarette dangling from his mouth. He replaced the lighter, and took a deep drag, relishing the sensation.

An old lady shuffling past gave him a filthy look. Glancing around, he noticed the *No Smoking within Five metres* sign at the hospital exit. He measured the distance in his head and reckoned he was about six metres away, give or take. Colbert stared at the woman and shrugged.

"Asshole," she said, coughing as she shambled through a hanging cloud of smoke.

Chuckling to himself, Colbert dragged on the cigarette a few more times as he watched the woman trundle to a nearby car and drive off. A voice snapped his attention away from her.

"Oi, you that reporter?"

Looking around, Colbert saw the woman who had caused all the commotion inside the Minister's press conference earlier. "Who wants to know?"

Her face split into a wide grin, showing a mouthful of white teeth. She thrust a hand towards him. "Tarni. Tarni Tanner."

Colbert took her hand in his own and shook. "Col Colbert."

"Oh, yeah, I know all about you. You're just as bad as me. You dig into the truth and print it. You don't give a shit what people think."

"Thanks, I think?"

"I reckon you're not buying all this crap that the Minister has been spouting, are ya?"

Colbert smiled. "Not really. What do you know?"

"Oh, a lot. You wanna learn more?"

"Depends on what it is."

"The truth. The truth about what they're doing up there. I know all about it."

"Okay, you've got my attention."

Tarni glanced around, then shook her head. "Not here. Come with me."

Following along behind the younger woman, Colbert found himself on the edge of the tiny town and approaching a run-down shamble of a house. It was an old timber worker's cottage that had been patched together with sheets of cast off and rusting corrugated iron.

STEPHEN HERCZEG

"Yeah, it ain't much, but it's been home for as long as I've known it."

The inside of the house had seen more attention than the outside and reinforced the small and simple nature of the building. A main room served as kitchen, dining, and lounge, while a doorway led off to a bathroom and probable sleeping area. A smouldering fire lent the house a comfortable warmth that chased away the chill from outside.

The walls held topographical maps and an evidence board full of newspaper clippings and photographs with string linking pieces of information to each other.

Colbert stared around the living area, his jaw working in amazement. "You certainly have a bug up your butt about this dam project."

Standing with hands on hips and a proud smile on her face, Tarni stared at her handiwork. "Yep. These city folk think they are dealing with some dumb palawa, but I did my study at the university down in Hobart." She pointed to a framed certificate on the far wall. "First in my family to graduate. Got myself a Science degree, in chemical engineering and applied mathematics. I'm no dummy. I know what they're doing in that valley."

"They're building a dam," stated Colbert. "Aren't they?"

Smiling wide, so that her dark face was split by the white grin of her teeth, her eyes sparkling with excitement. "That's what they tell everyone. Even the Minister's in on it." Moving across to the map, Tarni pointed out the location of the dam. "This here's where they're building the dam. It's just downstream from the confluence of the Gordon and Franklin rivers."

Col nodded. That was known to anyone who'd read the press releases. He stepped up to the map and pointed to the proposed location of the dam wall. "Yep. And the hydro station will be further downstream."

Pointing to a large red dot that had been added after the map was printed, Tarni said, "And this is the Tantangara Cave." She pointed to a blue dotted line. "This line is the proposed extent of the captured water."

Colbert nodded, then jabbed at another dot just north of the blue dotted line. "What's the significance of that?"

"Ah, that's what this is really all about." Tarni moved away and stepped over to the evidence board. She pointed to a more detailed map showing the area around the cave. "A few years ago, a geological survey was done of this area by a corporation from Sydney."

"So? That's fair enough."

"That corporation has links to both Novak Sujdovic and the Minister."

"Okay, what did the survey reveal?"

"Ah, that's where it gets very interesting." Tarni pulled a poorly scanned report from the wall and handed it to Colbert.

He stared at the blurry words and shrugged. Disappointed, Tarni pointed halfway down the typed page. "This is a mineralogical report that came from that survey."

Colbert focused on several of the words in the list. "Niobium, tantalum, scandium? Yeah, minerals, so what?"

"Rare earth metals. Valuable on today's market. They are used in the production of wind turbine components. The major source is China and Africa."

His eyes widening in realisation, Colbert said, "Right. If you could source those locally, you could slash your production costs."

"And if you did it on the sly, you could still charge your customers the same inflated amount as imported goods."

"But how would they set up a mine so that no-one knew about it?" As he stared at the map, the penny dropped inside Colbert's mind. "Holy crap. You put the mine entrance in the middle of an already established cave."

"That's right, and if you run the extraction operation during the construction phase of a massive dam, then no-one would realise what was happening. Plus, you can leave the tailings at the bottom of the dam and not remove them. Within a few years after you've finished mining, the whole thing would be covered in gigalitres of water and nobody would ever know."

"That's brilliant." He noticed Tarni's disapproving face. "And really wrong. But what's it got to do with the dead body?"

"What dead body?"

Realising he'd just let the cat out of the bag, Colbert searched for a way to change the subject. A voice croaked out from the corner of the room. The reporter glanced across at what he'd thought was a chair covered in blankets.

An old, wizened face peered out from under a colourful knitted shawl. "It has awakened."

Tarni stepped across to the old lady, and crouching down, she placed a loving arm around her. "Auntie it's okay, there's nothing to worry about."

Ignoring Tarni, the old woman opened her watery eyes and stared up at Colbert. "It has returned. They have awakened it."

"What?" asked Colbert, approaching the old woman's chair, and crouched down to her level too.

"The Pioial. It has always slept in the Tantangara Cave. It allowed our ancestors to live in the area in harmony. But now it is awake, it will only sleep when it feels safe once more."

"Auntie, don't get yourself worked up. There is no Pioial, it's just a legend, nobody's even seen one." Turning to Colbert Tarni asked, "This body? What of it?"

Colbert explained but left out the gruesome details. He finished with, "The Coroner reckons it's just a disagreement between blokes out at the dam site."

"See Auntie. Just men being stupid, as men are."

The old woman glanced at Tarni. "Don't be condescending to me, girl. I walked that land before the two of you were even considered. I've seen things that no other on Earth has seen. If I say it has awakened then believe me. Where is your respect?"

Admonished, Tarni rose and taking Colbert by the arm, led him towards the door.

The old lady sang out to them. "Stay away from the cave. The Pioial comes in many forms, most of them monstrous to our eyes, and it will not sleep until the danger has passed."

Outside, the sun had set, and the harsh chill of the Tasmanian mountains had descended. "Don't worry about Auntie. She's old, and she's pissed off."

"You don't believe her story about the monster?"

"The legend? Of course not. I'm educated. Those old ways are long gone."

"But you are trying to save the cave."

"I don't care about the cave. I don't like the idea that those bastards in suits are gonna make millions when us locals won't see nothing."

Colbert laughed. "Ah, it's all about the money then."

"Damn straight it is."

The sun's last light glimmered over the line of eucalypts in the west. Gianni wiped the sweat from his forehead and took a sip of water from his canteen before pushing on along the little dirt track that had appeared over the last few weeks.

Jesus Karrie, where are you?

When the young surveyor hadn't returned, Gianni's nerves had risen. Karrie had promised to meet him for a beer before dinner at the compound's mess tent. He had hoped that a single beer might turn into a few to get them into a more relaxed state and replay their liaison from two nights previous.

After asking around some of the other workers, Gianni was at a loss. No-one had seen her return. Karrie had said she would be photographing and mapping out the cave, so Gianni knew it would take a while. His main concern was that she'd get lost in the cave, or worse. After Adrian's death the other day the whole camp was nervous, but rumours spread quickly that Adrian had been killed by one of the local activists, and the cops were all over it.

God I hope they haven't returned and gone after Karrie.

That thought in his mind pushed Gianni along the little path until he finally saw the yawning mouth of the cave. Stepping inside, the faint glow of a work light illuminated the entrance. A carry bag and another collapsed tripod lay nearby.

She's been here then.

Pulling out a torch, Gianni scanned the area. "Karrie?" He called, his cry echoing through the silent cave, his own voice the only sound to return to him. Shivering as a chill ran up his back, he thought, "Keep forgetting how damn cold it is in here."

Crunching through the loose gravel on the cave's floor, Gianni hastened towards the rear of the main entrance. As he and Karrie had investigated this tunnel that led deeper into the bowels of the cavern on a previous trip, Gianni assumed she would have headed there.

Turning a tight corner, his torch revealed the larger cavern beyond. A snatch of light from across the open area caught his attention. Gianni switched off his torch and peered into the gloom, eyes darting from one side then back to make sure he was seeing it correctly and not just a residual image on his retina. There was light. It had to be Karrie. Turning on his torch again, he made his way between jutting rocks and loose stones to the source.

Reaching the other side of the cave, he shone his light on the floor, and gasped in shock. Lying on the floor was a yellow plastic hard hat, similar to the one he wore. Every member of the team had been issued with identical protective gear when they first arrived. Gianni tried to console himself.

It could be anyone's.

He picked it up and turned it around within the light of his torch. Seeing the nametag on the back, his hopes sank.

Karrie? But where are you?

Swinging the torch around, he frantically scanned the area. If Karrie's helmet was here, she shouldn't be far away.

She must be injured.

A sudden tumble of loose stones sent echoes through the cavern. Gianni twisted, searching for the source, hoping in vain.

"Karrie?" He called, his own voice cutting through the silence, drowning out all other noises. He *crunched* across the cave towards the source, calling his lover's name, unaware that the answering sound of grinding stones was approaching him.

His light fell on a large tunnel that led away from this central cavern. Calling out again and stomping towards it, Gianni's torch flew from his hand as a blinding pain shrieked outward from his torso. He cried out in agony, grabbed at the cause. Something was clamped around his midriff. Something hard and smooth.

Lifted off his feet, Gianni was dragged through the air, then turned to face his assailant. The wide beam of his torch shone onto the head of his attacker. Gianni struggled, the image burning through his mind. Eyes. Black, shining eyes.

A needle-like appendage moved in the light. A drop of liquid, shining golden on its tip. It flashed forward and Gianni's scream echoed through the cavern, escaping into the dark Tasmanian night.

"It's news Vincenzo, it's news." Colbert's hopes faded as he pleaded with his editor through the disconnected world of his mobile phone. This conversation was the latest in a long series of disappointments for Colbert.

"You can't print this, Col, you'll get us sued. Again." Colbert almost felt rather than heard the extra emphasis his editor Gabe had placed on that last word. "You've accused the Minister of collusion and fraud, for God's sake. If I print that, we're sunk. Even hinting at something like this without solid proof is a death warrant for a newspaper."

"Vincenzo, you know me, I'll get the proof. Keep the copy safe, I'll add to it when I've got definitive evidence."

"I know you, Col. Next you'll be talking about monsters or ghosts or some other stupid nonsense."

That comment hurt Colbert, he went silent for a moment, past memories coming back to haunt him.

"Col? You still there?" Vincenzo's voice dragged him back to the present.

"Yeah, I'm here Gabe. I'll get the proof you need, trust me."

"I don't trust you as far as I can throw you and given the crappy diet you've been on, that ain't far at all."

Looking down at the now silent phone, Colbert sighed. This trip was turning into crap, even though he knew there was something worth reporting on here, somewhere.

Pulling out his cigarettes and lighter, he lit up and took a deep drag, contemplating the hopelessness of his immediate future. His phone squeaked and vibrated in his pocket. Expecting another berating from Vincenzo, he dragged it out, hoping the ring tone would cut off as he did.

Glancing at a number he didn't recognise, he tapped the *answer* icon and put the phone to his ear.

"Hey, reporter man, you want a real story?"

Surprised to hear Tarni Tanner's voice, he smiled and said, "Yeah, what you got for me?"

After an hour of bumping and grinding their way along the goat track that had been carved out of the Tasmanian bush, Colbert was almost ready to pass out or return his breakfast to the wide world.

"Are you sure this is the right way?"

A wide smile greeted him in response. Tarni seemed to be enjoying herself as she wrenched the steering wheel in both directions and navigated another series of bone shaking ruts and mounds. "Mate, I've done this at least a dozen times now. You should have seen it before the hydro mob put this road in. It was a real goat track."

"It was worse than this?" Colbert asked as his teeth clacked together in another painful jolt to his system.

181

"Yeah, at least we can drive it now. Once upon a time it would've taken you half a day to walk out here. Hey, we're almost there, better pull off."

Colbert looked up and noticed a prominent collection of temporary buildings and tents off to the right-hand side of the track about a hundred metres ahead.

Tarni slowed to a crawl and edged the four-wheel drive to the left and into what looked like a purpose-built hiding spot.

"Did you do this?"

"Yeah, me and a couple of boys came out here a while back. Cut down some trees so we could hide a car away from prying eyes."

Stepping away from the truck, Colbert peered through the trees towards the compound. It looked quiet. "I'd thought there'd be police crawling all over this place," he said.

"Why? Isn't the dead guy in town?"

"Well yeah, but they need to find out who killed him. They should be interviewing the workers."

"They have. I heard they are now looking for some of those crazy activists. They think they're to blame."

Colbert nodded, then his eyes grew wider. "Hang on. You're the crazy activist. They'll be looking for you."

Tarni smiled. "Yeah, that's right. And anyone who's with me, I suppose."

Colbert swallowed against a dry throat. "Oh, crap."

Handing him a backpack, and putting hers over her shoulders, Tarni said, "Put that on, but be gentle."

Looking at the bag, Colbert asked, "Why? What's in it?"

"Gelly."

It took a moment for Colbert to decipher what the name meant. Then he almost dropped the bag in terror. "Gelignite? What the fuck is that for?"

"Hey, I told you I was gonna stop those bastards."

Colbert shook his head and held out the bag. "No fucking way. You'll get us killed. Or worse."

Pushing the bag back towards him, Tarni said, "You'll be fine. It's safe. Just don't light the fuse, that is." Laughing, she pushed past Colbert and headed down a narrow track that ran parallel to the road skirting the workers' compound. Staring at the bag for a moment, Colbert shook his head before putting the straps over his shoulders and hurrying after her receding figure.

An email ping echoed out from Novak Sujdovic's computer dragging him away from deeper thoughts about the impending mine construction timeline. Annoyed, he clicked on the entry entitled *GPS and site photo delay*.

The message had been sent to Karrie Silend, with Novak copied in as part of the ongoing policy. It was a question from the team performing the analysis and design on the mine entrance, asking where the promised photographs and GPS coordinate information had gone. The last sentence suggested that any further delay would cause a blow-out in the design timeline.

They should have got that last night. What the hell is Karrie doing?

The entire demountable structure shook when Novak rose and trudged across to the door into the adjoining room. Glaring across the space, he focused on Karrie's vacant desk. "Has anyone seen Karrie this morning?"

The three others working behind their computers looked at the empty desk, then back to their boss and shook their heads.

"Not since yesterday afternoon. She went down to the cave to take some photos or something," said a dark-haired man.

Novak held his sarcasm in check. "Yes, I know that. I sent her down there."

The man fell silent, looked around then went back to his work.

Pulling out his phone, Novak punched in a number and waited while the ring tone sounded in his ear. "Come on Gianni, pick up."

In the darkened depths of the cave system, a phone lit up, the shrill sound of a popular song blaring out through the silence.

Sujdovic's name danced across the screen as the phone continued to ring. A dark object crossed in front of the phone and clamped around it. The bright light thrown by the screen reflecting off the obsidian surface and flashing across the cave roof.

Then the area was plunged into darkness as the grip tightened, the phone cracking as it was crushed into a pile of useless technological debris.

Standing on the edge of the valley, Colbert and Tarni stared across the narrow gap into the heart of the construction compound. A temporary chain-link fence ran around the perimeter, with several large canvas tents and a couple of more solidly constructed demountable buildings.

"There's about ten on the team, with more to come. They flew the demountable buildings in with these huge helicopters, the rest of the tents came on the back of those land rovers over to the right." Tarni said, pointing to several machines on the far left of the compound. They looked like oversized power drills. "See those things? They are mining drills. They can be used to take small samples from a rock face. The excuse is that they are testing the strength of the surrounding bedrock, but my contact told me they've been using them deep in the cave."

"Your contact?"

"Yeah, you don't think I worked all this out just by myself. I've got a friend inside. She's not happy about what's going on but stays because of the money." Tarni smiled. "She says it's too good to pass up. Good for her, I reckon, but that flow of money's gonna stop pretty soon." She stood, hefted her backpack, and headed down the faintly visible path into the valley.

A fine line of white smoke wafted into the afternoon air. Novak drew on his cigarette and exhaled a thick cloud, blasting the fine line into oblivion. He was surprised how easy it had been to pick up the habit again. Most of society frowned on smokers, and as a prominent businessman he'd withdrawn his love of cigarettes to comply. But the stress of running this venture, coupled with the green groups, indigenous activists, lobby groups, politicians, and average joe blows all howling for his blood over something so trivial, had forced his hand.

Dragging another deep hit of nicotine into his lungs, he relaxed a little more, blew another stream of smoke into the ether and smiled. It was such a simple pleasure from a simple vice. He could have turned to drink and women, but past experience kept those desires at bay. Seeing the cigarette was almost finished, he took one last draw and dropped it to the ground, crushing it into the dirt beneath his work boot.

Looking up, he noticed movement and a flash of colour against the deep green of the foliage below. He concentrated on the figures as they advanced along one of the tracks that criss-crossed the valley.

He didn't recognise them as members of his crew, and the direction they were heading brought a stirring of anger into him.

Fucking activists. Have to be.

Glancing around, Novak saw one of the shotguns they'd secreted around the compound. Over the last month there had been a few devils enter the camp and forage through the garbage. They were harmless but could get vicious if cornered. The guns had been brought in as a deterrent to the devils.

Picking up the gun and a handful of shells from the nearby ammo box, he stormed to the path leading out towards the cave.

"Why am I here again?" Colbert asked, as they trudged through the bush towards the Tantangara Cave.

Tarni glanced back towards the sweat-covered reporter. "You're here to witness and report on the destruction of the cave."

Colbert stopped and gaped at the "What? You've got to be kidding me."

Turning around to face him, Tarni shrugged and raised her hands. "What did you think the gelly was for?"

"I thought you were going to blow up some machinery or something." He paced around, putting a hand to his forehead. "That cave. Isn't it an important cultural site?"

"Yeah, but not enough to stop those assholes from digging it up, or even just flooding it." She sighed, her head dropping in dejection. "You mob, you'd dig up Uluru if you found gold underneath it."

"Well, I wouldn't but, yeah you're right. Some would. But why blow the cave up?"

"Only the entrance. The rest will be fine. If those bastards want to use it as a cover to go after the minerals, they'll spend half their time digging out the cave mouth. By the time the valley floods it will be too late."

"Okay, I think I get it now."

"And—" Tarni poked Colbert in the chest "—if you do your job right, the Minister and the Hydro Corporation will be too busy covering their tracks. They might even have to can the whole project."

"I still think it's a long shot. They are bound to blame you."

She shrugged. "They already think I killed that engineer, so it's only natural." She stepped closer and smiled. "Besides, I'll have you to act as my witness."

"What?" Before he could say any more, Tarni turned and walked off down the path. Colbert watched her walk and debated whether to head back to the truck. He had the backpack full of gelignite, without him, her plan was sunk.

Over her shoulder, Tarni called out, "If you want the Minister and that sleazy Mr. Sujdovic to make a lot of money right under the public's nose then turn around, or I could always get myself caught and tell them that you were my accomplice all along."

His eyes growing wide, Colbert swore under his breath, and hurried after Tarni.

Stepping into the cave entrance, Tarni cursed, "Bugger, there's someone else here."

"How do you mean?"

She pointed to the work light. "I doubt anyone would leave one of these on. It's a two hour round trip to get batteries." She stepped over to the light and held a hand near the back. "It's hot, so they've been here a while. Probably pretty deep in the cave system. That stuffs up my plans."

"Oh, well, shall we just go then?" Colbert was hopeful he could get out of this without any more legal concerns sitting over his head.

Instead of turning around, Tarni pulled a torch out of her backpack and headed deeper into the cave, moving the light from side to side.

Colbert took off the backpack with the gelignite and placed it next to an abandoned backpack. He glanced at the discarded pack. "Hey, there's a name tag on this bag." He turned the tag over and read the name. "Karrie Silend? Know her?"

"Did you say Karrie?" Tarni's voice echoed back from deeper in the cave.

"Yeah," Colbert yelled back, "The backpack's tag says Karrie Silend." He stood up and peered through the gloom towards the activist. "Why?"

Tarni's voice became quieter. "She's the contact I told you about." The crunching of footsteps growing quieter filtered back again, followed by Tarni shouting into the depths of the cavern. "Karrie?"

Colbert stared into the darkness, unsure what to do next.

I should just piss off.

Taking two tentative steps back towards the entrance, Colbert stared at the various paths winding their way across the valley floor. His shoulders slumped as he realised he had no idea which one they'd come by.

Fuck. I'll just get lost and die in the Tasmanian wilderness.

Turning back, Colbert pulled out his phone. "May as well get some photos, then." Taking several shots of the cave mouth, he turned on the torch and started to follow. "Hey, Tarni, hold up."

Just as he stepped forward, the phone began to ring. Selma's number appeared on his screen. "Selma?" he answered.

"Hey, Col, I just got the tox screen back on that engineer. Thought you'd like to know the results."

"Of course, thanks. I'll owe you one."

"Yeah you will. That dinner you owe me sounds good."

"Okay, then. Might not be tonight, I'm out of town."

A disappointed voice replied back. "Fine. The poison was scorpion venom, a massive dose."

"Scorpion venom? How the hell did that kill him?"

"It wasn't the venom on its own. His internal organs had suffered massive damage."

"Damage?"

"Yeah, they were almost liquified. As if they were dissolving. If I didn't know better, I'd say the venom came from an actual scorpion, along with its digestive enzymes."

"That's ridiculous."

"Yeah, I know, the only thing I can suggest is that someone extracted a lot of natural scorpion venom, which would account for the enzymes, apart from that I got nothing else. Unless it's a bloody big scorpion."

"A big scorpion?" He looked around at the nearby forest, and then at the dark, suddenly foreboding presence of the cave. "Must be huge. How the hell would you kill it?"

"I usually use a rock."

Colbert looked down and picked up a large fist sized rock, he stared at it and grimaced. "Okay. I'll call you when I get back to civilisation."

"Do that."

Cradling the shotgun across his left arm, Novak worked his way down the steep and slippery pathway that his workers had carved out of the bushland. He cursed himself for not taking time to change into his heavy boots, the light treads on his current pair struggled to grip in the slimy mud created from the recent rains.

Music filtered up from the valley floor. Novak stopped and listened.

A phone?

The sound came from the direction of the cave. Stealing himself, he hurried on.

Picking his way across the rocky floor of the cavern, Colbert crept towards the tunnel he'd seen Tarni disappear down moments before. His phone barely lit up the immediate area, causing him to trip over protruding rocks and almost lose the phone several times. "Tarni?"

"Keep coming. Take the left tunnel at the end of the cavern."

Finding the entrance to the tunnel, Colbert peered into the gloom and saw Tarni's torch slash through the darkness. "Coming."

Approaching Tarni, she bathed him in the brilliant white light of her torch. "What the hell you got that for?" She asked, the beam falling on the rock in Colbert's hand.

"The phone call. It was the coroner. She said the engineer had been killed by a scorpion." He looked at the small rock in his fist. "This was for protection?" he said, not sure of his decision now.

"If it is a scorpion, you're gonna need a bigger rock."

Confused, Colbert's gaze followed the torch beam as Tarni swung it across the floor and illuminated another body lying nearby.

"That's not?"

Tarni shook her head. "No, it's not Karrie. I think this was her boyfriend or at least friend. I met him once. Name's Gianni something. Ran the campsite."

The bright torch gave the body a washed-out ashen appearance. The man's skin was drawn back as if he'd been dead a while and been dried out by the elements.

"Look at that," Tarni said pointing to a wide blood-crusted wound on the man's neck.

"That's different to the other body. It's messy, like it's been chewed," said Colbert.

193

Running the light down the man's body, Tarni found another wound in the man's chest. It was smaller and circular, with blood around the edges.

"That's more like the guy in the morgue. Coroner said it was a stab wound, where the venom was injected."

"Maybe the same killer got him, and some devils got in here later and ate him."

"That works."

Holding his phone out to try and take a photograph, Colbert stepped backwards. His foot collected something on the cave floor and sent it skittering away. Colbert turned and scanned the floor. The bright beam followed, highlighting a camera lying a few metres away. Quickly rescuing the camera, Colbert examined it in the light.

"It's on. Still got some battery left." A bright white flash burst across the cavern as Colbert pressed the shutter button.

"Shit," shouted Tarni, rubbing her eyes.

"Did you see something over there by the far wall?"

Tarni played the torch beam across to the area. A flash of red fabric showed between a pair of rocky outcrops. "You're right."

Forgetting about the body, they both moved towards the flash of red colour. The torch played across the area, highlighting another sallow face.

Tarni gasped as the second body was revealed. "Oh, Karrie."

"Your friend?" Colbert tried to sound sympathetic, something a little alien to him.

Moving the torch beam across Karrie's body, Tarni dropped to a knee and felt her friend's neck. "Cold, damnit. At least there's are no bite marks." She moved her torch to Karrie's chest and scrutinised a small puncture wound there. "I didn't know Karrie that well, but I liked her."

"Then why did you kill her?" An angry voice asked from the darkness behind them.

Tarni and Colbert stood, torches shining in the direction of the voice, bathing Novak Sujdovic in light.

"Jesus." Colbert said, raising his hands at the sight of the shotgun. "You don't need that; we're not armed, and we're not dangerous."

"Tell that to the dead bastard back there, and that poor woman."

"We didn't do any of this. Whoever killed your engineer did it."

"That was you." Novak pointed the gun towards Tarni. "You've been trying to get this operation shut down since day one. Couldn't do it legally, now you're desperate. Killing Adrian didn't do anything, he'd already finished his job." Novak took a step forward. "But, killing poor Karrie and Gianni, that's just annoying."

"Like we said, we didn't kill them," said Tarni, "We found them like this. You've got a killer running around poisoning people."

"Poison," spat Novak. "That poor bastard back there had his throat slashed." He lifted the gun and stepped closer. A crunching sound echoed out from the gloom behind Novak. "You've got a helper then?" He shouted at the noise over his shoulder. "Stay where you are, or these two are dead meat."

Gravel crunched several more times as something large approached from the dark. The light shone off its black carapace and glimmered off its twelve bulbous eyes. As it stopped only metres behind Novak, the giant scorpion spread its pincers wide either side of the man. The stinger rose high above Novak's head, a single drop of liquid hanging from the tip, ready to dispatch the man before it.

The rock fell from Colbert's hand, thudding to the ground. "Holy Christ," he gasped.

"Auntie was right. Pioial has awakened," said Tarni.

"Sujdovic, you need to move, now!" Colbert urged.

"I've got the bloody gun. I'll give the orders." He raised the gun to shoulder height and aimed between the pair. Looking back over his shoulder, he yelled, "Just stay where you are or these two will die."

The scorpion darted forward, its pincers lashing out and grabbing Novak around the chest and abdomen. The stinger shot out, jabbing deep into the businessman's back. He shrieked in pain, finger jolting back on the shotgun trigger. The roar of the gun in the cavern confines was deafening.

Tarni fell backwards as the pellets sprayed her. The torch bounced away, coming to rest against a rock and shining back at the massive scorpion. The creature withdrew its stinger and raised the paralysed man to its mouth. The gun came loose and fell, rattling to the cave floor.

Dropping to his knees, Colbert shone his phone's light across Tarni's body. Blood dribbled from several wounds across her chest. She groaned and tried to sit up.

"Good, you're not dead. We need to get out of here." Colbert put his phone in his jacket pocket, with the torch shining out. The young woman groaned and cursed at him as he hauled her up and onto his shoulder. He trudged his way across to the nearby tunnel and into the main cavern, but skittering footsteps echoed from behind him. Colbert turned and the light shone on a jet-black pincer as it reached out towards him. "Fuck." He moved as fast as he could towards the cave entrance. Tarni groaned and yelled in pain as she was jostled and tossed about.

The wash of clean air from the light breeze blowing into the valley was a welcome relief as Colbert reached the cave entrance. He stepped out towards an open area and lay Tarni on the sparse covering of grass.

The sound of crunching gravel from the cave caused Colbert to spin around. Movement within the cave revealed the giant scorpion as it lowered itself to the cavern floor and stepped towards them.

Where the hell did that come from?

Scanning the immediate area, Colbert realised they had no hope. He'd never be able to carry Tarni away from the creature fast enough. As he spun back, Karrie's camera bumped against his chest. Grabbing it, he pressed the power switch and popped up the flash unit. Raising the camera as he stepped inside the cave mouth, Colbert pointed it at the scorpion and pressed the shutter release. The flash ignited, flooding the cavern with bright light.

The scorpion squealed and backed away into a darker area of the cavern. Buoyed by his success, Colbert pressed the button again. The flash ignited, sending the scorpion further back into the cave. Stepping forward, Colbert pressed the release button again. Nothing. Pressing it again, the camera clicked then went silent.

Fuck. The battery.

Sensing its attacker was weaponless, the scorpion edged forward. Its pincers clicked and clacked as it approached Colbert.

Spinning back towards the entrance, Colbert's eyes fell on the dimming work light by the cave wall, and then down to the backpack beneath. He sprinted to the pack, snatched it up and ran from the cave.

He dropped to his knees, pulling out his lighter, and unzipped the bag's main pocket to withdraw the bundle of gelignite.

Christ I hope this works.

The fuse sparked and flared almost immediately as it ignited. Confused, Colbert stared as the fire approached the body of the explosive he and laid, he hoped he had been right about all of them. Fear growing, he stepped back towards the cavern and threw the sticks of gelignite as far into the cave as he could. The orange flame of the fuse shone off the scorpion's body as it tried to scuttle further away in fear.

Running back to Tarni's prone body, Colbert knelt down beside her, shielded her from the blast. The explosion echoed across the valley. The remaining workers in the compound above the valley ran outside to see the dust cloud spread across the tree canopy. Many residents in Strathgordon stepped outside and searched the heavens with dismay for an approaching thunderstorm.

Back near the cave, Colbert coughed and spat out a mouthful of limestone dust. He glanced around at the pile of rubble that had once been the entrance to the Tantangara Cave. There was no sign of the scorpion, no signs that a cave had ever existed, only a crumbling wall of rock and stony debris.

Shouts and voices filtered down from the compound. Through the veil of trees, Colbert saw movement as several people began the descent.

Shit. Need to get out of here.

Grabbing at Tarni's hands, he pulled her into a sitting position, but the young woman groaned. Her eyes fluttered open, then squinted at the light. "What did you do to me? How much did I drink last night?"

Smiling, Colbert replied, "Not as much as we'll drink tonight if we get out of here." Helping Tarni to her feet, Colbert said, "There are people coming. You know the way out of this hellhole, I don't, so wake up now."

"I'm glad you're worried about my health," she said, choosing a pathway and shambling towards it.

It's news Vincenzo. News.

As Colbert read his finished story, he imagined the conversation with his editor. The same one he'd had countless times before. The same one he knew he would have for many years to come.

Closing the computer file, he dragged it into the specially protected folder. The place where all the stories that were never going to see the light of day ended up.

The Pioial or *The Giant Scorpion of the Tantangara Cave* would only destroy his fragile career. He planned to finally resurrect it after he retired, but even then knew it would only ever be seen as a piece of fantastic fiction.

He quickly read the puff piece that would end up on his editor's desk. It described the accidental destruction of the heritage site. Colbert had revisited the cave and interviewed several workers. They claimed it was an accident, caused by explosives stored in the cave and a burnt-out work light. Colbert kept his amusement in check as the official story was told from several different angles.

Nobody ever mentioned the missing co-workers and Chief Officer, and there was certainly no indication of any giant arachnids.

As far he was concerned, Tarni and he were safe from official interest. All the evidence that they were even there was buried inside the cave. Whether there was enough to indict either of them was something to worry about at a later date.

The last hours of the previous day were still fresh in his mind. Tarni had remained conscious enough to lead them back to the truck. Colbert had then driven them to her auntie's house where he could finally have a good look at the young woman's wounds.

She'd been lucky. The shot had winged her, the damage mostly coming from falling backwards onto the rocky ground.

Her bulky vest had absorbed much of the pellet damage, with a few small wounds that bled enough to confuse his first inspection.

Along with a rich knowledge of the local lore, Auntie Kirra was a retired nurse and was able to treat Tarni's wounds without the need for other medical intervention. When Colbert had related their tale to Kirra, the old woman had smiled and nodded. Saying only that the Pioial would never be found. It came because its home was threatened, and now that time has passed, so has the Pioial. Colbert wasn't convinced and expected any future excavation of the site to reveal the huge monster. Though details from the morning's press release indicated that the cave would be left alone as the dam construction was accelerated.

Colbert's understanding of the news item was that a certain Government Minister may be trying to hide his own involvement in the project now that his business partner had disappeared.

Scanning once more across the news piece, Colbert ran a spell check, then compiled an email for Vincenzo. As he pressed the *send* button, his phone rang. Selma's name appeared on the screen.

Smiling, Colbert snatched it up and answered.

About the Author:

Stephen Herczeg is an IT Geek, writer, actor, film maker and Taekwondo Black Belt from Canberra, Australia, who has been writing for well over twenty years, with sixteen completed feature length screenplays, and numerous short and micro-fiction stories. Stephen's scripts, TITAN, Dark are the Woods, Control *and* Death Spores *have found success in international screenwriting competitions with a win, two runner-up and two top ten finishes.*

He has had over fifty short stories and seventy micro-fiction drabbles published through Hunter Anthologies; Things In the Well; Blood Song Books; Dragon Soul Press; Oscillate Wildly Press; Black Hare Press; Monnath Books; Battle Goddess Productions; Fantasia Divinity and Deadset Press.
A growing number of his Sherlock Holmes and H.G. Wells inspired tales have found favour with Belanger Books and MX Publishing.

He lives by the creed "Just Finish It", and his Mum is his biggest fan.

You can catch Stephen at his Facebook page:
https://www.facebook.com/stephenherczegauthor

THIS IS THE DAWNING
(PART XI)

Helena McAuley

Virgo's blood erupted as Scorpio tore him apart. It sprayed onto Doug's face, warm and wet. He froze, trembling, unable to speak, unable to even comprehend what he'd just witnessed.

"Douglas," Capricorn's voice was hard and flat. "Run."

Somehow, he managed to comply.

As his feet smacked the pavement, he felt the pressure of mind-speak but was unable to form the presence of mind to hear it. A moment later he was no longer running alone. To his left was Leo, and to his right was Pisces. Both were effortlessly keeping stride with him, their faces taut and grim; an honour-guard of superhuman protection.

Doug risked a glance over his shoulder at the dwindling form of Capricorn, but he couldn't make him out. He stumbled, and was caught by Leo, who set him back on his feet.

"Just run," he said; his tone, like Capricorn's, conveying a calmness that was inexplicable under the circumstances.

Doug turned his eyes forward and redoubled his efforts. He didn't need to be told again.

I don't watch Douglas leave. My eyes are fixed on Scorpio.

He shifts his weight, adjusting his balance, and then draws his tongue across his lips, tasting Virgo's blood.

My jaw clenches and I strike. The emanation burns from my hand, but I have fallen for Scorpio's goading. He merely leans aside before bringing forth an emanation of his own. I counter, and my yellow light meets his with the sound and smell of lightning. His emanation—as it has been for as long as I have been incarnate—is titanium-grey.

Scorpio was not always thus; a gleeful instrument of destruction. Once he had compassion and rationality. Like poison through veins the darkness crept into his being, twisting his mind, stilling his heart. I do not know what happened to create this perversion of his once steady self, but at this moment I don't care.

I am keenly aware that we are in the open, in the daylight, amongst homes and families. I have to keep Scorpio's lust for destruction fixed on me, or else it may spill out onto these homes, these families, these children. Let the humans see. Let them think what they wish to think, create whatever urban legends they will create. With Virgo's cooling blood still on my face, I don't care about that, either.

He is unable to overwhelm me, and I him. He breaks first and launches at me with fist raised. I lean back and grasp his arm in both hands, pulling and guiding him as I twist aside to throw him to the ground. He rolls across his shoulder and is on his feet in an instant, firing a short burst of titanium energy into my chest. It lifts me high, but I steady myself in the air and return to the ground. Scorpio is fast; he has always been fast. He shoots forward and buries his fist in my stomach.

I wrap my arms around him, crushing him to me as if to crush his bones, and bring the crown of my head down on the bridge of his nose. It may rattle him for a moment, if I am lucky, but not for long.

This is pointless. His physical blows cannot truly harm me, nor mine him. The true battle is not physical, but one of will and intention. A contest between the grip I have on my form and Scorpio's desire to eradicate it. No harm can come to me, except through the overpowering of my will by another's, just as Scorpio overpowered Virgo. Through each battle the question remains the same; is my will strong enough to withstand the assault?

Is it enough to defeat what Scorpio has become?

For the first time in my existence, I am not certain.

I cannot unmanifest, lest he lose interest in me and fail to follow. I cannot unleash myself here, not so close to so many humans—to Libra and her children. And while Scorpio may not share my reticence, he seems unwilling to strike me down, preferring to toy with me as we dance around the bones and organs of what was once our fellow.

Enough. Still gripping him, I take to the sky, and though he struggles and resists, we are kilometres away by the time he breaks my hold. He falls, briefly, before regaining himself and shooting towards me in a vain attempt to knock me from the air—an attempt that is much easier to avoid than on the ground.

"You want me?" I shout to him. "Come and get me!"

His lips twitch into a leer. I have his full attention now. Good.

I leave him, moving just under the speed of sound, but I know he is following. The ground far below us becomes an incomprehensible blur as the city begrudgingly gives way to trees, fields, and then mountains. I descend and allow my feet to rest on the alpine soils. I am struck by the silence and smell of the trees. I do not have the time to appreciate it; Scorpio lands a moment after me, and I attack.

He is prepared. My emanation hits a tree and the silence is split by a deafening crack as wood explodes into splinters and the tree falls. As soon as his position is revealed I take aim, but he moves first, and I only have time to twist my body before the spear of dark-grey energy lances through my shoulder, puncturing muscles, severing sinew, and drilling through bone.

That is more like it.

My mind reaches into the earth, not out of rage as it was yesterday, but out of desire. I pull at the threads that bind the land, coaxing and coercing with my force of will. Sagittarius and Aries have their fire; Libra and Gemini their gale; Pieces and Cancer their torrent. I—like my fallen brethren—have this.

The ground erupts, lifting and sagging as if the tide has come to the mountain. Rents appear in the ground and the trees are ripped from their homes. I ride the waves as a boatswain rides out the storm, and Scorpio tumbles down the now perpendicular soils. As he nears an expanding fissure, he sets his feet against the edge and launches at me, we meet in an embrace and topple together.

I plant my feet in his abdomen and push as I roll, sending him flying upside down into the trunk of a great fallen snow gum. The movement sets fire to my injured shoulder, but I will deal with the wound later. As I surge to my feet I reach again for the threads of the earth, but Scorpio is reaching for his element also.

The very moisture from the air condenses and coalesces and hits me with the force of a tsunami. I am battered back, sliding for several hundred meters, tearing a furrow in the ground and leaving decimated bushes, shrubs, and trees in my wake.

These poor trees. They did not deserve this.

A second blast takes me, and I tumble through the storm, drenched to the bone, battered and bruised. Were I human I would drown in this. How amusing it would be for others to try and fathom my death; a man drowning on the top of a dry mountain. But now is not the time for humour.

Even as Scorpio prepares another wave, I unmanifest and pass through the squall, regaining my physical form behind him. He turns and the heel of my hand connects with bone, snapping his head back and streaming blood from his nose. Good. I aim my emanation at his chest, but it meets with a defensive field of metallic energy. I turn it aside and cut downwards instead, burning through his leg, turning the flesh to ash and exposing bone. He bows and grits his teeth but does not scream, then he responds in kind. I have no time to bring my defences to bear and his emanation tears into me, ripping apart one of my kidneys.

As I stumble back, he hefts a bough, undeterred by his injuries, and ploughs it into my ruined side. I crumple with the force of the blow. I bring my hand up to strike again, but he plunges the bough into my chest; splintering the wood and puncturing my lung. The length of wood tears through my back like a burning fist and I cannot stop the scream that rips from my lips and echoes through the silence of the mountain. He releases the shaft and I am left swaying from the weight of this new addition to my body. I grip it with one hand, but it is stuck firm.

Listing to one side, my hand lashes out and grabs a fistful of his matted dreadlocks. He tries to pull away, but I hold tight and bring his head to my chest as a father may do a child. The protruding bough pierces his eye socket and is buried deep. The sickening squelch of brain-matter giving way is my reward, as is the scream that tumbles from his mouth; transmuted into a moaning howl from lips and jaw left slack.

I unmanifest, excluding the bough so it drops to the ground. The bough is brought forward by the force of Scorpio's weight and it bursts free through the back of his skull; the fibres of the wood peeling back and splaying like a bloodied flower. But even this does not end him. As I retake my physical form, I am impressed by the level of command he has over his; it is almost comparable to mine. A body so controlled by will that mere physical attack has no lethality.

No matter. I grasp him under the arms, feeling the ribs coated in a thick layer of sinewy muscle, and summon my emanation; an indefensible, killing strike.

Yet it meets nothing. Scorpio is gone. Unmanifest from beneath my hands. I turn, scouring the devastated mountain top for his presence. Nothing. He has fled, kilometres away in that instant, to lick his wounds.

I release a breath turned into a growl from my bitter frustration. And then, though I should be able to counter it, my physical body turns to shock and I am left alternating fire and ice from the core of my being. The tremors overtake me. I am too unrested; the exertions have been too much.

I collapse into the dirt, surrounded by the whisper of the wind and the quiet song of tentative birds, witnessed by nothing more than a cold, cloudless sky.

Doug's head was heavy in his hands as he sat bowed on Pisces' couch. The air was thick and heavy with forced calm as Leo, seated next to him, and Pisces, brewing yet another round of tea, projected light-hearted indifference. It was for his benefit, he knew that. He also knew that it was a waste of their energy. Even the most callous glance would recognise the softly spun tension in their casual movements; too slow, too gentle, too calculated to give the best impression of ease. They were taut with the burden of waiting. Doug knew this, because he was taut, too.

He glanced at the window, watching the twilight drain from the day. Stifling a growl, he bowed his head back into his hands, pulling at the tender threads of hair at his scalp.

Pisces set fresh tea before them, lifting the near-full, cold mugs from the table and whisking them away to the kitchen.

Doug stared at it, an ungrateful sneer on his face. Peppermint, not dandelion and chamomile, but still, he couldn't stomach it. He turned his head towards the kitchen. "Are you *sure* he's not dead?" he asked, again.

"Very sure," her voice sang back. "He's not responding to me, but I can still sense his presence. He's alive—somewhere."

"Why doesn't he come back, then?"

"He may still be dealing with Scorpio," Leo rumbled.

Pisces tensed at the name. "Or perhaps he is injured and attending to his wounds?"

"Then we should be looking for him!"

Leo shook his massive head. "Pisces and I are to keep you safe."

With a sigh, Doug sagged back into the couch, his eyes fixed on the ceiling. This level of worry was draining, as was the inactivity of simply waiting. Pisces' home—usually so warm and welcoming—was too still, too silent. The silence became a near tangible object, a fragile blanket that had settled over them, so that the miniscule sounds of the house threatened jump-scares—the tick and cool of the kettle was a gunshot; the inconsistent hum of the fridge was saw-teeth through the silence; even the whisper of cloth as Pisces cleaned the immaculate kitchen was as grating as sandpaper.

Doug squeezed his eyes shut, his jaw aching from being clenched too long. But when he closed his eyes, he saw Virgo; the fear in his dark, wide eyes, the tremor of his colourless lips.

The look of shock on his face as he was torn apart.

With a gasp, Doug's eyes flew open again, greeted by Pisces' off-white ceiling. The mundanity of it allowed the memories to fade, and his mind traced the wavy edging. The sawing of the fridge started again, shattering the blanket of stillness.

He turned towards Leo, who was running sausage-like fingers through his beard and also staring at nothing.

"I'm sorry about Virgo," Doug said, his voice a gentle murmur, barely audible over the chainsaw of the fridge.

Leo's eyes lost their glaze and fixed on him. "It is very bad form to destroy the incarnation of another outside of the Dawning."

Doug couldn't think of a response, and anyway, he'd had enough. The interminable waiting and worry were more exhausting than their flight from Scorpio and the panic that had overtaken him soon after. Everything felt tense; his muscles, the silence, even the very air felt stretched too thin, like an elastic band about to snap.

He stood. "I'm going to bed." Pisces gave a warm smile and a nod; Leo only grunted an acknowledgment. Doug stalked to the spare room, kicked off his shoes and jeans, and crawled under the covers.

THIS IS THE DAWNING (PART XI)

It was not much better in the bedroom. He lay awake staring at a ceiling bisected by moonlight, and again saw Virgo's face. What a horrible way to die. Is that what was in store for him, come the Dawning? Was this what he had signed up for?

He didn't want it. He didn't want any of it. Lazily he raised his hand and called the corposant blue flame. It was comforting, and though he could feel it lick his fingers it did not burn. It was almost cool, like ammonia evaporating from skin. He watched the blue flames dance, waving his fingers and turning his palm, and the tension in the air relaxed. This, at least, felt like it belonged to him, in a way he had never felt anything was his before—not his arms, not his legs, not the hair on his head. It felt like an extension of his being, an extension of his very mind.

He lifted his hand higher and willed the flame to expand, falling around him as a curved barrier, as if he were encased in a protective sphere. It cast its own light in the darkened room, brighter than the moonlight, yet softer, more welcoming. There were flickers within the pale light, electric points fine as thread, brief and brilliant meteors in the stratosphere. Doug watched them, mesmerised, until his shoulder started to ache.

When he lowered his arm and bid the blue flame to vanish, the room felt lonely, but peaceful. Doug sank into the calm and finally allowed his muscles to relax. He lay, watching the steady crawl of the moonlight across the ceiling and listening to the sounds of the house, no longer gunshots or chainsaws, just creaks and groans—and a fridge.

The last tendrils of restless energy fell away, and with it, Doug's grip on the waking world.

Day turns to night and I remain on the mountain top, rebuilding my broken body. The shoulder is simple, the chest wound more trying. As for the abdomen, well . . . That is still a work in progress. Cell by cell I stitch myself together, an exercise in patience more than will. As the hours leak by, I become strong enough to stand, strong enough to function. Not for the first time in the last hours I feel Pisces reaching out for my mind. I ignore her. The lack of panic in her query is enough to tell me they are safe. For now.

I unmanifest. But I do not go to them.

The rooftop on which I retake physical form is slanted and tiled. I sit and gaze across the night-cloaked street, and I see *her*. Libra. The blinds to her home are undrawn and the warmth cast into the night illuminates a contented family. The children are in warm pyjamas, husband and wife nestled on the couch together; he watches a screen, she reads a book. Her husband is bespectacled and narrow set—not frail, but not robust. He has not changed from his dress shirt and suit pants.

My nose crinkles. I cannot fathom Libra being with this man. I cannot fathom that he could withstand her desire and drive.

Vaguely I am aware that Virgo's body is gone, the path washed clean. Unlike the site of Gemini's end there are no signs of investigation. Have they finished? Or was it taken care of before an investigation could begin?

I failed him. Just as I failed Gemini. Just as I betrayed Taurus. This existence, once so static and calm, is now riddled with regret. My efforts all lead to failed ends. I reach into the earth and feel the threads there, caressing them, not cajoling. Mother Earth grieves for the future of her children. As do I. But is there not a chance? Or am I destined to fail in every endeavour?

"I thought I might find you here." The voice behind me is kind and yet snidely humoured. "You're becoming predictable, Capricorn."

I grit my teeth. "Leave me, Sagittarius."

She bends her lithe form to rest on the roof's edge, next to me, but just out of arm's reach. "No," she says. "I don't believe I will."

Her gaze follows mine to Libra's home, to the comfort she has found there, to her family. "She looks happy, doesn't she?" The wistfulness in Sagittarius' tone ends the warning threat on my lips before it can blossom. When I do not respond, her eyes flicker, downcast. "I'm sorry about Virgo."

217

"It is of your making."

"No, Capricorn, it is of yours," she fires back. "*You* killed Taurus. Aries and Scorpio acted in retribution. You have taken this obsession too far. Abandon it."

I turn to her, eyes narrowed. "You agreed to the plan."

"And the plan has failed."

It is the authoritative weight to her tone that silences me. Failed? Perhaps it has, as all my efforts have. Perhaps the tremors of the Earth are not fear, but warning. Perhaps, perhaps, perhaps . . .

"No." I reply, and my tone is firm. "It has not. Not yet."

"Look around you! Look at this mess called humanity! You believe your scheme will save them? It will *destroy* them, Capricorn. They are not ready."

"Aquarius will *make* them ready," I counter.

"Aquarius isn't even incarnate."

Again, I have no rebuttal for the truth. He is not Aquarius; only Douglas. Not for the first time I try to fathom *why*. After all he has seen, after all he has experienced, *why* does he not remember? Why does he not incarnate? Why does he choose to slumber?

Sagittarius stands, her voice taking a milder tone. "I will extend my hand only once."

I do not meet her gaze.

"Stubborn goat," she sighs. "Remember Thálassélas," she tells me, and then is gone.

Remember Thálassélas.

If only I could.

The lights in Libra's house are dimming, her children and husband taken to their beds. I watch each light wink out as she takes one final tour of her home and ascends to the bedroom. At the window she grasps the curtain but pauses, and her eyes flicker to mine. Her face is unreadable across this distance, as I am sure mine is also. There is neither irritation nor longing in her. Of all my failures, of all my regrets, this is the one that cuts the deepest. She draws the curtain, and I am left alone.

I do not bother to stand, merely melt into the aether and allow my physical form to depart. It is not even a moment before I arrive in Pisces' living room, but I do not manifest— not yet. Pisces and Leo are there, each silent and still, neither required to speak. That is one trait of our kind; we are very good at waiting. And yet, I witness Pisces' nervous tension, and the waves of anger and grief that roll from Leo. Neither are of my design, and yet both are of my making.

I turn away.

I pass through the walls and find Douglas, asleep. In the darkened room I reassert my being and watch him; the rise and fall of his chest, the flutter of his eyelids and the slackness of his lips, the ease of sleep that erases tension from the body. Not Aquarius, but Douglas. Perhaps forever to remain so.

Why won't Aquarius come to my aid?

The weight of sorrow is overwhelming and I collapse onto a decorative chair beside the bed. My grief is a physical sensation, a pain in my chest far greater than being skewered by a tree limb. This body of mine, once so utterly controlled by my will, is reasserting itself in ways that are all too *human*. Perhaps my will is failing me. Perhaps I have remained incarnate too long.

Perhaps. Perhaps. Perhaps.

Douglas twitches in his sleep, a snuffling intake of breath and a crease to his face before he shifts and settles. As I stare at him my bitterness melts away and is replaced by a startling truth.

I would die for this boy. Wrapped in all his human failings and juvenile ignorance is a fathomless well of optimism and hope. Humanity may be broken, and I may have contributed to the breaking, but here before me is one worth saving.

I would die for this boy.

Not because he is Aquarius. But because he is Douglas.

Before I can contemplate that further there is a shift to the air. It is as if every atom and molecule has turned on its side. The cresting wave of tension that has built for days breaks and succumbs, pouring into the material realm. Flooding it.

Washing away the restless waiting and leaving a lagoon of clear, sharp, *action*.

With a curtailed gasp Douglas sits upright in bed and my head snaps towards him. His eyes are glazed, unseeing.

"It is time," he breathes.

As if experiencing a second awakening he turns towards me, the drowse leaving him as he affixes me with an intense stare. He does not seem surprised by my presence.

"It is time," he says again.

My jaw clenches. I nod once.

"Yes," I say. "It is."

To be concluded in the next edition of the Zodiac Series— *Sagittarius* . . .

HELENA MCAULEY

About the Author:

Helena McAuley has been the recipient of such prestigious literary awards as "Most Likely to Lose her Myki", "Mistaking a Rosella for a Cockatiel", and "The Premier's Award for Literary Incompetence".

This is, of course, a joke. As if Helena would ever win a literary award.

And yet, she has been published in various ASF anthologies, Williamstown Writers anthologies, and a fortune cookie that she hand-wrote and managed to stuff into the biscuit before it broke. When not writing or breaking food safety regulations, she can be found – and now it's your turn to hide.

'This is the Dawning' is a serialised debut that will be published throughout the ASF Zodiac series. This is it. This is the actual Dawning. Will Doug and Cap bring about the Age of Aquarius? Or will the forces of Sagittarius prevail? Find out in the next anthology!

Helena (mostly) twits, (sometimes) instas, and is (rarely) facebookified under the handle @thathmc

Note: It's a sting in the tail to be a scorpion, but it's good fun. Without it, you'd just be an amblypygid.

ABOUT AUSSIE SPECULATIVE FICTION

Aussie Speculative Fiction is a recently established group which was created to support and promote Australian speculative fiction writers.

Check out our links:

www.facebook.com/Aussiespeculativefiction/

www.twitter.com/aussiefiction

www.aussiespeculativefiction.com

www.books2read.com/rl/asf

ABOUT DEADSET PRESS

Deadset Press is the publishing imprint of Aussie Speculative Fiction—a community aimed at supporting Australian and Kiwi authors. You can learn more at:

www.aussiespeculativefiction.com

#

The Zodiac Series

Capricorn (The Zodiac Series #1)

Aquarius (The Zodiac Series #2)

Pisces (The Zodiac Series #3)

Aries (The Zodiac Series #4)

Taurus (The Zodiac Series #5)

Gemini (The Zodiac Series #6)

Cancer (The Zodiac Series #7)

Leo (The Zodiac Series #8)

Virgo (The Zodiac Series #9)

Libra (The Zodiac Series #10)

Scorpio (The Zodiac Series #11)

Sagittarius (The Zodiac Series #12)